Of Goats and Poisoned Oranges

A novel by Ciku Kimeria

Self-published by Createspace – a subsidiary of Amazon.com Inc.

First published in December 2013

Third reprint (i.e. Fourth print) – February 2021

ISBN-10: 1494275856

ISBN-13: 978-1494275853

www.thekenyanexplorer.com

Happy families are all alike; every unhappy family is unhappy in its own way.

- Leo Tolstoy, *Anna Karenina*

For my parents – Lucy Wangui Kimeria and the late Philip Macharia Kimeria, who always encouraged me to dance to the beat of my own drum.

Contents

Prologue, The Year 2013 1

Chapter 1: Nyambura, The Year 2002 7

Chapter 2: Wambui, The Year 1978 13

Excerpt from Sunday Nation Feedback section, August 10th 2013 21

Chapter 3: Njogu, The Year 2002 22

Chapter 4: Nyambura, The Year 2002 27

Chapter 5: King'ori (Njogu and Wambui's son), The Year 2011 31

Chapter 6: Njogu, The Year 2000 40

Chapter 7: Nyambura, The Year 2001 46

Chapter 8: Wambui, The Year 2005 50

Chapter 9: Wambui's sisters on a call, The Year 2009 57

Excerpt from Capital FM News, September 13th 2013 61

Chapter 10: Nyambura, The Year 2003 62

Chapter 11: King'ori and his cousin Wandia, The Year 2011 65

Chapter 12: Nyambura, The Year 2012 71

Chapter 13: Wambui's sisters on a call, The Year 2012 74

Chapter 14: Njogu, The Year 2012 79

A few words of wisdom from the wise 82

Chapter 15: Nyambura's sister, The Year 2013 84

Chapter 16: Nyambura, The Year 2012 86

Chapter 17: Muriungi (Nyambura's brother), The Year 2012. 93

Chapter 18: Wambui, The Year 2013 95

Chapter 19: Njogu, The Year 2013 100

Chapter 20: King'ori, The Year 2013 102

Chapter 21: Njoroge (Wambui and Njogu's Mr-Fix-It), The Year 2013 110

Chapter 22: King'ori and his cousin Wandia on the phone, The Year 2013 116

Chapter 23: Nyambura, The Year 2013 119

Chapter 24: Wambui's cleaning lady, The Year 2013 121

Chapter 25: Wambui, The Year 2012 125

Chapter 26: Njoroge (Wambui and Njogu's Mr-Fix-It), The Year 2013 128

Chapter 27: Wambui and Njogu, The Year 2013 130

Prologue, The Year 2013

It really is a strange situation to find oneself in – that of attending your own funeral. If anyone had told me that the day would come when I would get to listen to my own eulogy, see old lost friends shed a tear for me and notice the absence of those I had assumed would be at my funeral, I would have thought them mad. The questions running through my mind at this moment may appear trivial given the circumstances, but they are gnawing on my mind nonetheless: Who chose these funeral colors – Njogu knows how much I hate red! How could they omit my greatest accomplishments from the eulogy – you can never trust people to do things for you! Who is that woman sitting on the second pew with the ridiculous hat? Nearer my God to thee? Who is responsible for this lack of originality at my funeral? You always live your life expecting that the day they lay you to rest will be unique. That the tears people shed for you will be more than they have ever shed before. That the eulogy will be a perfect rendition of all your successes. That the sun will stand still and the moon will stay in place as it did in the bible when Joshua went to battle. Bollocks! All of it. In reality, your funeral program will have typos, villagers will scramble for a copy to display on their walls, the professional mourner might put up a good show, but it will all fall through when in the midst of her pretend-sorrow, she howls out the wrong name. The old lady next to her will remind her, "Wambui. She was called Wambui." It is true what was said, "This is the way the world ends, not with a big bang, but a whimper."

Two weeks before my death

I would like to say that this was like any regular day. That I went to work, came home after work and spent a lovely evening with my husband. The end of the day is true, but the rest of the day followed a slightly different pattern. I did go to work and made a huge show of greeting everyone as usual to ensure that when police asked them any questions about my behavior prior to my disappearance, they would say they had noted no significant change except a hint of melancholy. At around 10am, I left the office feigning a terrible headache and said I was going to the doctor. I jumped into my car and it took me a good hour or so to get from Lavington to the city center. Traffic was a headache. A truck had stalled on the road – regular case of unroadworthy century old trucks being unable to get up a hill. Twigs behind the truck signaled its untimely demise, and the rest of us were stuck to maneuver round the little space left by the truck. At 11am I got to Dr. Owuor's office, and picked up my letter indicating that I was quite ill and would be spending the rest of the day on bed rest in his clinic. Dr. Owuor was that type of doctor. The type who gave you letters indicating you were too unwell to travel, if you needed to miss a flight – and were not keen on paying a $50 fine. The type of Doctor who a few years ago, had not batted an eyelid when we brought in my 16 year old niece who had gotten herself into a little bit of trouble with a boy, and needed a discrete way of ridding herself of the unborn child who would surely be an impediment to her college plans and plans of eventually marrying a doctor – like Dr. Owuor. By noon, I was waiting in the reception of some shadowy building in River road. It is one of the streets in the city center that a lady of my caliber does not particularly enjoy finding herself in, but sometimes in this life we have to deal with discomfort for the greater good. Five minutes later Njoroge arrived. He opened up the brown envelope. I took out the new passport and identification documents in it. Everything checked out. The picture was mine but instead of reading "Jane Wambui Njogu", it read, "Peris Wanjiru Mwangi." I took out my purse and handed over the KES

100,000 balance I had to pay for my new identity. It was worth every shilling! I went home and feigned spending a lovely evening with Njogu resenting the fact that I was stooping this low because of his actions.

Six months after my death

The investigations went as planned. My distraught 80 year old mother showed the police the texts I had sent her. The texts mentioned Njogu's mistress – Nyambura – and how my life was becoming a living misery because of her. I had told her about the death threats from Nyambura. The constant harassment I faced as she kept on threatening to come public with their relationship. The sleepless nights. The constant fights with Njogu. My sisters, my chamamates[i], my friends all corroborated that story. They painted a picture of me as the perfect wife whose life was shattered by the imperfect mistress. With further investigations, the police were able to find several bank transfers to Nyambura in my name. It was an open and shut case. Nyambura had grown weary of waiting for me to die, waiting to finally have direct access to Njogu's millions. She had grown impatient and killed me. She thought it was a perfect crime and that no one would suspect her. She had been sloppy and my bloodied clothes were found buried in her backyard – in the lovely home in Kileleshwa that Njogu had bought her. Though my body was never found, she was sentenced to life imprisonment in Langata Women's prison. Her manicured nails and her long weaves would do her no good here. There was finally justice for me.

One year after my death

Life was not all rosy living in Dubai as Peris Wanjiru Mwangi. I had stashed away enough money in the past years to be able to live comfortably for at least two years in Dubai, but I missed my family – who wouldn't? Bit by bit I began to fear that I might never be able to carry on this façade forever. I knew I had taken a big risk by traveling to Kenya for "my funeral", but I knew I had to do it. I needed closure. I needed to see that my plan had worked perfectly, but most of all I needed to look at the faces of my loved ones and see what they felt at that point. I had to fight the urge to run and hug my distraught mother as she tried to follow the empty coffin into the ground. A bit of me died when I saw my only child – my 30 year old son, crying – completely inconsolable. Only a mother can relate to the pain of watching your child suffer and being unable to comfort them. Fear ran down my spine any time I bumped into other Kenyans. It would be impossible for them to recognize me, but that did not make it any less worrying. What if I met someone I knew and they recognized my mannerisms? My voice? The plastic surgeon had done a brilliant job, but the fear of recognition still lingered. I remember at the funeral when my cousin stared at me, walked straight up to me and asked who I was. I almost choked, but I was able to quickly remember my line, "I was a good friend of Wambui in Alliance high school. When I saw the obituary in the newspaper, I decided to come and pay my condolences. She was such a nice person..." She agreed, "The Lord giveth and the Lord taketh. She is in a better place right now." That phrase always annoyed me. For all we know, the dearly departed could be slowly roasting in Hades as we speak. Well, it was good to know that I had tested my new face, and it had passed the test.

One and a half years after my death

I knew this moment would come, but my intestines entangled as soon as I boarded that Kenya Airways flight back home. One and a half years is a long time, and so much changes. I was also a new person now and would have to remember that. No more stopping old friends on the street if I met them in town – I was not me. No more picking up my phone and saying, "Hello, Wambui Njogu." Wambui Njogu was dead, and I had to be Peris Wanjiru Mwangi – a Kenyan who had lived in Dubai for over a decade and had decided to move back home so as not to miss the African revival sweeping through the continent.

I took a taxi from the airport all the way to the leafy suburbs of Karen that I had called home for close to two decades. Chaotic traffic gave way to wider open roads the closer we got to Karen. One could always tell how posh a neighborhood was in Kenya by the presence of sidewalks. The rich have sidewalks and every now and then you would pass a jogger or someone walking their dog. The rest of the country mostly has no sidewalks, and pedestrians had to make do with squeezing their way in between hawkers, stalls, cars and motorcycles. I paid my fare, walked out of the taxi, fumbled around in my handbag until I found the house keys. I opened the door, walked into the large entryway of our mansion. I was glad to see that everything was in place. Njogu must have kept the cleaning lady. I leaned against the wall in the living room – happy to feel the cold on my cheeks. It felt so good to be home. I stared at all the pictures on the wall – a walk down memory lane of the life we had shared for over 30 years. Memories flooded into my mind, and I felt a tear roll down my cheek. I walked into the kitchen and found leftover matumbo[ii] on the kitchen counter. A twinge of jealousy came over me – Njogu must have had a woman over last night! The cleaning lady hated the smell of matumbo, and could not have been the one who made it. I had left the kitchen door slightly ajar. Suddenly it swung open, and there stood Njogu.

He ran over to me and embraced me. "Oh, my gachungwa[iii], I had missed you so much!" I lay limply in his embrace. When he released me, all my unspoken words found their wings and flew out in no order – like dragonflies before a storm. "I told you! How many times did I tell you! It is these young women who will finish you! The other ones – at least the other ones were compliant! They knew their place. They knew they were the mistress and I was the wife! They did not dare take their children to the type of schools our friend's children went! They stayed away from our church! This Nyambura bitch! You picked up a bartender, upgraded her, and she set her sights on my position! Calling me and telling me that we are co-wives! Me and a kinyangarika[iv] like that! Telling me that since you have a 10 year old son with her, she can go to court and demand some of your property! Does she know where I took you from? Does she know when I met you, you had jiggers? Does she know I was the daughter of a chief and I married beneath me! Does she know that you are what you are because I made you successful! Foolish woman! Thinking she could come and take my hard-earned wealth! My shambas[v] in Karen! The houses in Lavington and Runda! She had to pay! She had to pay! And you! Stop looking like you are so innocent! How many times have I had to come and clean your mess! How many times Njogu? You will be the end of me! I always told you it would be these young women who would bring us problems!

Chapter 1: Nyambura, The Year 2002

Love – that elusive force that most seek, but few ever find. Millions of libraries could be filled with all that humanity has written about romantic love (eros). Today I want to talk about oft overlooked love – the love of family. The love one has for the unborn child in their womb, the love one has for siblings who if it was not for a shared history, one might quite quickly forget. A cross between Storge (Affection) and Agape (Unconditional love). Ah yes, the reader wonders how love for family can be unconditional. Especially in the African sense where family encompasses blood relatives, those related to us by marriage and in many cases those of unclear, unknown or perhaps even questionable kinship to us – Your uncle's secret lovechild with his neighbour's wife. We definitely do not love all our relatives equally – some we are indifferent to, while some make us question their real ancestry and others we can do without seeing except at weddings and funerals. For those we love, though that feeling is strong and even stronger based on the shared history, shared stories, shared kinship.

The more people we love though, the more we will grieve over (unless we go first of course). In which case, the more people love us, the more people to grieve over us.

I always knew I loved my mother. Love was not something much discussed in my home growing up, but it was something taken for granted. Of course, your parents love you if they kept you when you were born, fed you, clothed you, and educated you as best they could and so on. Of course you loved your siblings, as had anything ever happened to them you would not have thought twice of taking in their (many) children. Birth control really was not at the advanced stage that it is at in this day and age. What would anyone ever need six children for? But of course you would have taken them in – they are family.

When my father died peacefully in his sleep (he was always a peaceful man who did not want to bother others, and we would not have expected him to go in any other way), it was decided that my mother would move to Nairobi and live with me. She was strong as an ox, and had she had her way she would be tilling the soil on the foothills of Mount Kenya until she had arthritis, but we decided it was best not to leave her on her own. We feared she would be claimed by a phenomenon whose name we did not know, but which could only be best described as "consolation death." Old couple, rural home, one dies, the other follows in a timely order – usually one or two years after – so as not to burden the family with funeral bills too quickly and so as to have time to set other affairs in order – resign from village committees, visit grandchildren and impart last words of wisdom and secure title deeds for various plots of lands. Essentially closing the books on one's life to hand them over neatly to the life auditor.

My older sister was unable to keep my mother. She had quite a full house with her husband and their six children. My younger brother had always been a rolling stone, and we were not entirely sure where he was at this time, gathering no moss – as usual. All we knew was that he resurfaced once a year or so, told entertaining but always unbelievable stories of where he had been and what he had been doing, borrowed some money ("which he would definitely pay in the next week") and went missing until his next visit. My mother moved in with me, and it all started out very well. She was always a woman of many words while I was one of few words, so between us we had enough words to keep us occupied for a few years. At which point the anticipation was that new things would have happened in the world that would give us new things to talk about. It was ideal.

I was financially stable, and was earning a decent living. My first time moving to Nairobi close to a decade back is one I do not like to think about, but will sum it up as thus – the big city was not what I expected it to be. I came here to study for a diploma at a secretarial college after completing high school, but things did not work out as expected. My parents could not sustain me as I studied, and I took on a part time job. I told them I was working as a receptionist, but the truth was that I was a waitress in one of the more upscale clubs in Nairobi. I could not divulge my secret for my parents would conclude that I really was a barmaid. I was working nights, and selling more drinks than food, but I did like to think of myself as a waitress. The term "Barmaid" conjured up images of the biblical whore of Babylon in many Kenyans' minds. I am not quite sure who did this great disservice to the profession, but that was that and I was not about to reveal my secret to my family. Armed with my diploma after two years, I frantically searched for a job. Times were hard. University graduates were "tarmacking[vi]", core secretarial skills such as shorthand had been made irrelevant by computer keyboards and the new breed of Administrative Assistants (formerly known as Secretaries), were a polished lot with impeccable English, impressive CVs, worldly views and great looks. Compared to the specimens out there, I looked like a village girl in the city – which I was. I remained at my waitress job for quite a few years, until fate smiled on me and sent a man to take me out my misery. True love does conquer all.

By the time my mother moved in with me I was a rising member of the Nairobian middle class. I was a self-made business woman (ok as self-made as one could be in my circumstances). I no longer slept in fear wondering if I would be able to pay rent on time, send some money home and pay some school fees for my nieces and nephews. I was financially stable, and enjoying it.

My mother's problem began shortly after her fiftieth birthday. I had taken her to a favourite nyama choma[vii] place of hers on the way to Ngong Hills. My sister and her brood had joined. I paid the bill, but that was fine with me – I could afford it. We had driven there in my Toyota Four Wheel Drive and had enjoyed a lovely day of going down memory lane. It was a perfect sunny Sunday, no traffic, a few warthogs crossing the road – much to the children's excitement, lots of food and some wine for the adults. On getting home, I was warming my mother's evening tea in the microwave when she said, "Nyambura, I am so happy that Muriungi made it today." I was initially unsure of whether she was joking or being sarcastic. We had not heard from Muriungi – my younger brother – our family's rolling stone in over 8 months. I finally attributed her comment to the two glasses of wine from earlier in the day and thought nothing more of it. My mother had never been much of a drinker, and perhaps the two glasses of wine had gone to her head.

A few months later, another strange occurrence took place that made me realize there was more to my mother than what I was seeing. I had been out most of the day running errands, and came home to find my mother watching her favourite channel that aired Nigerian movies during the day. She told me that in my absence, my cousin Monica had dropped by and they had a great chat about her side of the family. She narrated to me anecdotes that seemed plausible, but somehow peculiar. Monica got twins? It was an open secret that she had been trying to get a child for a while, but one would have expected to have heard sooner. That is how the family rumor mills worked. We all knew who was pregnant, whose husband was cheating, whose daughter had run off even before the involved parties themselves were fully aware. In any case I was also surprised that Monica dropped by without calling me first, but I quickly forgot about it.

A few weeks later, I coincidentally bumped into Monica near Electricity House on Agakhan walk in town. Hugs were exchanged, the usual niceties and not so niceties followed suit ("You have lost weight", "You have gained so much weight") and usual questions about life in general.

"Congratulations about the twins! I am so happy for you and Makokha!"

"Hmm, What are you talking about?"

This was followed by a long and awkward silence.

"Mum told me you got twins."

"I have no idea where she got that idea from! Please stop discussing me in your home as if you have nothing better to do!"

She stormed off and I was left baffled. I was not sure what exactly had just happened, but I knew that the twins did not exist, and I was not sure that my mother knew that.

I was left with three options:

A: Monica lied to my mother (not altogether implausible. Monica lied sometimes to paint a better picture of her life, but why would she lie about something that could instantly be uncovered, and then deny it?)

B: My mother lied (banish the thought, Mum only told necessary untruths – "What a beautiful baby!", "Such a big house!", "No, this githeri[viii] is not burnt at all, it's quite delicious."

C: Mum believes that she saw Monica and that Monica told her she had twins

Of all the options, C was the most likely one, but also the most somber. The darkness had come, and now it would surely not leave us alone. It was a well-known but often hidden fact in our family, that we had a history of mental illness. It was often trivialized and talked about like a playful ghost. "Your auntie went mad and used to spend all her days talking to herself," "Oh, you don't remember your cousin Wangeci? The mad one who burnt all her husband's clothes?" Madness is the African catch-all phrase for all sorts of strange behavior including bipolar disorder, schizophrenia, and dementia among others. Though I did not know it at this time, my mother was caving in to dementia, and it would be a long journey from which she would never quite return.

Chapter 2: Wambui, The Year 1978

I did something that many might not have thought was a good idea at the time - I married a poor man for love.

I was back in Nyeri visiting my parents from University of Nairobi where I was close to completing my Bachelor in Commerce degree. It was a few days after my twenty first birthday. Though our home was in the countryside, I would not call it rural. Our house would have been very much at place in Tigoni or Runda. We were rich and lived an urban life in an idyllic rural countryside. Our houses stood on the top of the hill as a beacon to the rest of the community (houses as my father had three wives, and each had their own compound). Neighbours were awed by our automatic gate, piped water and all the other amenities that money could buy. My father liked to joke that he employed the whole village – which might have been true given all the workers at the three homesteads and the hundreds of acres of arable farmland we had. My father was the first born son of a Chief, and was therefore a Chief himself. During the Kenyan struggle for independence, we had been on the "right side" of the battle, and had sided with the mzungu[ix]. This was the way we had been able to keep our wealth and increase it significantly with the additional land we got from the Mzungu for our loyalty. Perhaps my father did not always sleep easy once we finally gained independence in 1963 and we were branded traitors, but money can surely buy enough security. He always reminded us of the other great chief and colonial loyalist who had been assassinated by the Mau Mau[x] in cold blood in 1952 in his car on his way to Gachie. This story was a constant reminder to us, that there was a price to pay for having reaped the benefits of colonial patronage. For the most part though, villagers' resentment of us had eventually waned when they realized that we were willing to share the spoils. So maybe my father was paying school fees for hundreds of children, and maybe we did not need as many workers as we had on the farm, but was that not a small price to pay to buy loyalty? My father always told us "Remember to help others. It will always benefit you to have people indebted to you. They might still hate you, but they will need you. To be needed is to have many in whose best interest it is to see you succeed."

My mother was my father's third wife. She was his favourite, and growing up we always knew that we had a special place in his heart. We were his retirement children – born at a time when no one would have thought him capable of siring children let alone being capable of performing the prerequisite physical act. Though my mother never gave him a son, he was sufficiently pleased with the three daughters she bore him. His affairs were in order and he was a forward looking man in that he ensured we would all inherit a portion of his property and never be marginalized by the sons of his other's wives.

Oh, yes. I was telling you about how I met Njogu. So I was visiting my parents from university. By this point my father was mostly senile, but we still followed the rituals of our home. In the past ten years, my father mostly spent his evenings at my mother's home much to the other wives' chagrin, as they felt she was probably trying to claim a larger stake on his wealth. We had a three course sit down dinner. He could not really hold his fork and knife, but was assisted by one of the servants. Drool kept on pouring down the side of his cheek, and it was sad to see a man who had always been a pillar of strength, reduced to such a state by old age and a series of strokes. It was just the three of us as my younger sisters were in boarding high schools in Nairobi. There was nothing really new to discuss so we mostly ate in silence.

The next day, my cousin, Kamau, picked me up for a day out in the town. He was always one of my favourite cousins, fun and so full of life. He was home visiting from the UK where he was studying. He had his father's driver for the day as his father was out of the country for a business meeting. We eventually went to the Nyeri country club for lunch. We requested a private room. He knew we would probably be drinking alcohol and in those days it was still highly frowned upon for a woman to be drinking in public, especially when not in the company of a husband or fiancé. Times have changed. Liquor was flowing, stories were getting funnier by the minute. Around 5pm, Kamau had to leave to pick up his fiancée. She was studying at a Teacher's Training College in the area. She preferred the personal touch of being picked by him rather than the driver.

Kamau said, "I don't want to leave you here on your own. I should be back in half an hour. Is it ok if I ask the driver to join you?"

"Yes, sure no problem. I am a big girl, but if it will make you happier..."

The driver, Njogu, turned out to be very entertaining company. I had made it a habit not to interact with people of the lower classes. One never wanted servants to get too familiar to you and begin acting like your equals. Lines had to be clearly drawn. Njogu was very funny and my walls came crashing down as soon as we began to talk. Till today I try to dissect how I got attracted to him, and I now think of it in three ways.

First, he was speaking to me in Kikuyu. Though I could speak fluent Kikuyu my station in life resulted in my speaking English. It was not explicitly thought that my language was inferior to English, but there was a general feeling that mastery of the English language was the preserve of the truly privileged, and we had to show it off as best as we could. I would equate it to being able to speak French in Victorian times in London. It proved you were worldly, that you had means to travel and had travelled or even better yet, that you had a Governess who taught you French. You were privileged. Speaking in my mother tongue to Njogu made me feel like a more "real" and "in touch" version of myself.

Secondly, he had no pretension around me. My name and my family always made men feel very inadequate. A few of the men who were pursuing me at university tried to impress me with money, flashy gifts, stories that hinted at "Look at me! I am exactly like you! I am rich too. We are a logical match!" Most of those men bored me as in impressing me they morphed into only slightly different versions of the same person. Conversations were all the same. In all honesty, even if they were rich, their wealth was cheap change compared to my family's wealth. It was hard to impress me with money, as I had always had loads of it.

Third, he was not immediately forthright in his pursuit of me. I am a humble woman, but I will readily admit that I have always been a looker. My good looks and my confidence always had me in high demand. Very few conversations with members of the opposite sex did not end up with effusive declarations of undying love or premature marriage proposals. It was interesting to see a man who I considered inferior to me, resist my charms.

At the point when I met him, I was not clear headed enough to think all this through, but this is what I know now. I have reflected a lot in my life as I was always asked, "How did you and Njogu end up together?" Even the question betrays the fact that most of those asking knew I was definitely the one who was in the position of power. I was the one who did the choosing rather than Njogu. I could have had my pick of any man, but I picked the pauper's son, the driver – Njogu.

For the rest of that week, I found more excuses to spend time with Kamau and his fiancée. In reality I was finding ways to see more and more of Njogu. No one would have suspected the immense joy our passing conversations brought me. No one would have suspected that my heart soared every time I saw him, my heart beat a little faster every time we spoke, I dreamed of him every night and counted hours till I would see him again. I realized that I had never really laughed until I met him. Of course I had laughed, but not in the way he made me laugh – aching ribs, tears rolling down my cheeks. I did not have to be a rehearsed version of myself when I was with him. I could be myself. On the day I departed for Nairobi, we exchanged postal addresses, and promised to write to each other.

His first letter arrived within two weeks of my getting back to college. I had contemplated writing first and then got nervous that I might come off as being over-eager. The first few days in university I could not eat, I could not sleep. I constantly kept on thinking about him – replaying our conversations in my mind, wondering if I was building castles in the sky. Does he really feel the same? What if he was just being nice? Fear turned into panic. Oh, my god, what if he was hit by a bus when crossing the road to the post office? Would Kamau tell me? Would he feel the need to tell me? I am never going to find love! Oh gosh, what if he has someone else? What if he has a wife and two children? These driver types can never be trusted! By the end of the week, panic had given way to bitterness. That is what you get for giving a driver a chance! Who wants a poor man anyway? I can do so much better. By the time I got his letter in two weeks, I was damn near maniacal. From the envelope, I knew it was him (ok his name was also on the address line on the envelope.) I sat on my bed, ripped open the envelope with shaking hands and began to read. It was in Kikuyu (it never dawned on me till later that perhaps he was not comfortable writing in his limited English). It read as follows:

John Njogu
P.O. Box 33521
Nyeri
20th March, 1973

Dear Gachungwa,

I hope you are fine. I apologize for taking a long time to write. There has been a shortage of stamps in Nyeri, and I had to travel to Murang'a on my day off to buy some. I am not sure where to begin. I have written several versions of this letter as I waited to find stamps and decided to keep the one that was most sincere.

I have not been able to stop thinking about you since the first day I met you. I wish you were here with me now, instead of me having to write this letter. I miss you so much. I hope you feel the same way too. I cannot forget the last night when I dropped you home, and walked you to the house. I wished sometimes that the car would have broken down before getting to your place so that I would have walked miles with you rather than a few meters. I did not know how to say goodbye. We held hands, I tipped my cap and watched you walk into the house. In another life, I would have kissed you. In another life, I would not have had to fear that your father would kill me.

I know your family will be disappointed in me, but I promise to be a good husband to you. What I lack in schooling, I make up for in hard work. I promise to always work hard and provide for you. I promise to keep you happy. I promise to always treat you like the queen you are my gachungwa.

I hope you will accept my advance proposal. I have started saving up and I am happy to start the traditional ceremonies and eventually walk you down the aisle in church. I have met the woman I want to spend the rest of my life with.

Yours truly,
Njogu

I did not hesitate to write my letter back.

Jane Wambui Maina
University of Nairobi
P.O. Box 31456
Nairobi

My love Njogu,

I am crying as I write this letter. My heart will burst with joy. I accept your proposal. Nothing would make me happier than becoming Mrs. Jane Wambui Njogu and sharing the rest of my life with the best, kindest, funniest man I have ever met. I will be a good wife to you, take care of you and God will bless us with many children.

I have never felt for anyone what I feel for you. You must be my soulmate, and my life is brighter knowing that I will always have you in it.

Yours truly,
Wambui

We were married a year later in a simple wedding ceremony in Nyeri. Simple in that the budget was small rather than simple in that there were few people attending. Hundreds of people turned up, many out of curiosity. Who is this unknown man marrying one of daughters of Maina? Njogu refused my parent's offer to pay for the wedding. He wanted to ensure that he was the provider from the beginning and that my in-laws would not say that he was a "kept" man or marrying me for my money. The one concession he made was in agreeing to have the ceremony on our expansive property. Otherwise the rest of the wedding was according to his budget. There is a Kikuyu saying, "Mundu ethuaga haria egwikinyira" that means "One scratches themselves where they can reach". Njogu was determined to only scratch himself where he could reach and not have anyone assist him. It broke my family's heart to see me marrying a man who was not from a prominent family, but now that I had found love, I was not going to let myself marry for anything other than love. Love truly is a beautiful thing.

Excerpt from Sunday Nation Feedback section, August 10th 2013

I think it is easier to get back to someone you know than moving on and starting over with a stranger. In my view, repairing a leaking roof is easier than building a new house. It is reasonable to hate someone who hurts you in love, but nothing hurts more than seeing someone you love, love someone else. It has been said that experience leaves us wiser and I agree. There is a man who cheated on his wife with 21 women and when his wife was asked why she was still with him, she said she was stronger than them because he always came to her each night. To me this story depicted a determined and proud owner of something special that lures her husband back to her.....Sometimes in love you only have two choices, you live with it or you change to fit in.

Chapter 3: Njogu, The Year 2002

You know the strange thing, I cannot really remember the first time I cheated on Wambui. I am not a Lothario. Far from it. You know what really irritates me these days? The West constantly trying to change any infidelity into a sort of disease. Oh, Tiger Woods had a sex addiction. Oh, this other guy was not hugged enough by his mother. No, the bear just got caught stealing some honey and got stung! Let me tell you one thing I have learned in my several decades of marriage – monogamy is a myth. There is a reason our ancestors were polygamous. Oh, women? Women are created for monogamy. A man though, he is a lion! He needs to prey, to stalk. Man cannot live on bread alone, and a wife no matter how wonderful she is can soon turn into bread – constant, unchanging. It is good to know you can always have bread in case you are hungry, but it is even better to know that you can have something other than bread every now and then.

I am a very simple man. The wealth I have now was not something I would ever have expected to have. I grew up poor, dirt poor. My father was a cobbler and my mother was a housewife. Between them they had eleven children (each joined the union with children from other relationships). I was the seventh born of eleven children. I am what I can best describe as "slightly educated." Some schooling touched me, but did not really stick. Putting food in my belly always took precedence over learning different tenses. I dropped out of school in standard three. I was always good with numbers, but mostly because one needed to be able to count their cents, know how to earn enough from odd jobs to survive and so on. Though I still lived at home, I can say I was essentially self-sufficient from the age of ten. I am sure our parents cared for us, but there were too many of us. In a house such as mine, one grew up quickly. Several odd jobs later, I had a comfortable job as a salaried driver for Wambui's uncle. That is actually how we met. I do not remember the specifics of it, but I knew that this was my woman. Another man in my station in life might have faltered, but I have always been good at female psychology. I knew that she liked me, and I liked her too. To be honest I loved her. I think I still love her. She is one of the only two women I have ever loved (three if I count my mother). I am not sure I ever loved my siblings. It was hard even as a child to see them as anything other than competitors for the limited resources in our home.

Our marriage started off well, but it was definitely not a bed of roses – or maybe it was – considering how thorny it became. Her family detested me for nothing other than my poor upbringing. They felt that my family was a stain on their family's good name. My family was overshadowed even at the wedding. Many guests left the wedding believing that my siblings must have been servants at the Maina home. They were all in their Sunday best, but what is a Sunday best with loads of mileage when compared to the best? It was definitely not a marriage of equals. In Wambui's defense though, she did everything she could to treat them as equals in the beginning. After our wedding we moved to Nairobi, where Wambui had secured a comfortable job in a Government Ministry. True to my word, I worked hard to be a provider. Armed with a natural entrepreneurial spirit and Wambui's wealthy connections I was soon in business. What type of business? Everything. Diversification must have been invented in Kenya. I have my hand in cement, coffee, flowers, chicken feed, sugar, anything. You name it. Where there was money to be made, Njogu was there making it. In time I had my own money, but what I could never get was the honor of having old money. No matter what I did, I was always going to be seen as Wambui's husband – the one who used to be a driver. No matter how much I made, I was never going to ever be able to speak without betraying a problem with my R's and L's - a symptom of a life spent speaking in my mother tongue, with no mastery of the English language. I was always going to die a little bit inside when we spent thousands on a meal, and I thought of all my struggling relatives in Nyeri. I was always going to feel like a fraud having a driver – knowing I used to be a driver. Wambui was always kind, but mostly in a manipulative way. She tried as much as possible not to act as if she has clutched me from the jaws of poverty before I was chewed into a pulp, but she had her moments.

"Njogu, tell my friends again that funny story of how you used to walk five miles to school barefoot, and you once met a leopard."

Her friends - African versions of British housewives, "Gasp, really?", "Wow, That must have been so scary!", "Heeeee, you have come from far!"

Always reminding me that I had come from far, but I was still so far from fitting in with their high class bourgeoisie lifestyles, their trips abroad as children, their perfect English.

Wambui was always the perfect planner. When we moved to Nairobi she supplied me with a more suitable group of friends than the ones I had. It all started with little comments, but soon I realized that there was a script, a role and little deviation from the script was acceptable.

"Njogu dear, that friend of yours. What's his name? The mechanic. Yes, that one. I don't like how he cleans his teeth with the toothpick without covering his mouth. I think we shouldn't invite him for the next dinner."

"Njogu, I think some bottles of whisky are missing. Do you think it was those guys you had over the other day?"

Bit by bit, I slowly alienated anyone who did not fit in well with the new image I was trying to create. My old friends from Nyeri were quickly replaced with the husbands of Wambui's chamamates and friends. They were all generic. If you had met one you had met all the rest.

"Oh, yes, I got these cufflinks in London. In the same shop that my wife loves to shop in."

"Remember those awful mashed potatoes and minced meat we used to eat in high school?"

We still tried to be charitable because Wambui always felt the need to help out even those she felt were inferior to her. Our assistance was cosmetic though. Poor visiting relatives were placed in the guest house and did not join us in the main house for meals. Bed sheets were sanitized and dishes sterilized after their departure for fear of the maladies the poor could bring. My parents only visited once, and I do not really like talking about that time. What was even worse than Wambui's false kindness was my own false kindness. I felt ashamed seeing them walk into our house barefoot, with dirty sacks of produce they had brought for us.

People began to talk about me, and word always got back to me. "They are saying you are "sat on[xi]". "They are saying she has your balls in a jar." I resented these comments, but also feared that they were true. "Uthuri wa gitonga ndunungaga" is a Kikuyu saying that translates to "The rich man's fart does not stink." Was I the poor man who was forced to pretend I could not smell the rich man's fart?

As I said I cannot tell exactly when I started cheating on Wambui, but I know it was around three years into our marriage, when the cracks in the foundation of our marriage begun to widen. I always came back home to her. Ok. Almost always. Until I met the other woman I love.

Chapter 4: Nyambura, The Year 2002

I am coming to terms with it. My mother has dementia. She however is having a very hard time coming to terms with it. I think it would be easier for her if she was always demented (I hate that word, makes her sound like a serial killer or something), but the challenge is that she has bouts of normalcy punctuated by terrible episodes. When she is fine, she will tell all her lively stories. When she is unwell, she will descend into a dark place where no one can reach her, not even herself. The best I can do is talk to her even when she is not making sense and try my best to be cheerful. I am not sure if that is what a doctor would recommend, but she has adamantly refused to see one, with the same agitation a drunk person has when they are told they are drunk. I tiptoe around the issue and pretend that everything is normal though we clearly know it is not.

I preferred it when her hallucinations were about happy things – people visiting and others having babies. The other day she said "Nyambura, I need to tell you about your father." I thought it would be something mildly unpleasant, but easier to deal with e.g. "He had other children, He was a closet alcoholic." My father had always been the image of virtue and therefore even such a scandal after his death would do little to change the opinion I had of him. I tended to do that a lot – rarely change my opinions of people once I liked them or detested them, even if evidence on the contrary popped up. In all honesty, I do not believe in people being either good or bad. I think there is a lot of grey area, and as long as you are on the right side of grey, I am willing to consider you good. So it turned out that my mother's confession was going to be a disturbing one. She said, "Sometimes he visits me from heaven and we talk."

"What do you talk about?"

“The usual things. Who has he met there? Who is he surprised to have not met there? When will I join him? Did the repairmen finish fixing the leaking pipes in the drip irrigation system? Who is taking care of the shamba? The usual...”

“Ah. Ok.”

A few days later she was having one of her “normal” days. She whispered to me in a conspiratory tone, as if the walls could hear her, “I am so blessed to have a daughter like you. Do you know how many old people are left on their own because their children consider them a burden? No, no, Nyambura, do not start to cry. I just want to let you know that we have always loved you. We know things were never easy for you once you moved to Nairobi. Things did not work out for us, and we wanted to support you but we could not. I know you have probably had to do things you are not proud of to get where you are. Do not let them define you. Please do not start crying my child. I do not want to make you sad. I just want to get some things off my chest before I go. You know I have to go. I cannot live forever. I am going mad. I know I am. I have days, weeks that I cannot account for. Whatever you do, get a child. Please get a child. I know there is a man, but you do not bring him to me. I cannot judge you. It is your life. Get a child for when the darkness takes over your life. Someone to nurse you and help you down this last road as you are helping me. We Kimani women, this is how it ends. At least I made it to fifty. I had a full life. So what if I went mad towards the end? Just do me one favor. When it is my time to go, and it will be my time to go very soon – do not try to hold me back. My work on Earth is done. By the way did I tell you about what your great-grandmother said to me yesterday?....”

That was the last time we had a real conversation. After that the bouts were more and more intense. She would become emotional, angry, depressed, and there was little I could do to help her. Eventually she was bedridden. Despite her protests, I got a doctor to come see her. His diagnosis was that dementia had given way to depression and there was little he could do to help her. Her current affliction was more of the heart than of the body. She wanted to die. That night I cried like a baby in the living room after having made sure she was asleep. I could not cry in my room as I feared she would hear me, and I did not want to add any more pain to her last days. I was mourning in advance.

My mother had always been an avid churchgoer, but given the current situation it had been a while since our shadows had darkened that hallowed hall. A few weeks before she was bedridden, she had asked for us to attend what would eventually be her last church service. In true Presbyterian fashion, a somber sermon was read, visitors were welcomed and some visitors from Scotland were also bid farewell. A most peculiar hymn was chosen for their departure. "God be with you till we meet again," a funereal hymn posing as a farewell hymn. I believed it was a foreshadow of things to come. At one point my eyes met my mother's eyes, and we both quickly looked away as if we had glimpsed what the other was thinking and realized that we were thinking the same sad thoughts.

A few days before my mother's fifty first birthday we invited Muthoni (my sister), her husband and their six children and my brother Muriungi who was coincidentally back from one of his jaunts. The mood was somber. We never quite said it but everyone knew that at the end of the day when they said goodbye, this was going to be their last goodbye to our mother. Muriungi, never one to acknowledge feelings, kept us laughing with stories of his adventures in Malawi,

Mozambique and Zambia. We all laughed even though we were not really paying attention and even though we barely knew what was truth or fiction. We laughed in that forced "let us laugh otherwise we will cry" type of way. My mother was frail but mildly cheerful that day with her progeny around her. After everyone left I gave her, her evening tea and she said, "There are three men on the roof knocking. Do you hear them?"

That was the week she began her hunger-fast. I do not really tell anyone about it, as it was a private ritual for both of us. I would bring in her food, she would pretend to nibble at it, and I would clear the dishes. She knew I knew, and I knew she knew I knew, but I took this to be the message she conveyed when she said, "When it is my time to go, and it will be my time to go very soon – do not try to hold me back." She had decided to take matters into her own hands, as Death and his three horsemen companions seemed to be stuck in Nairobi traffic jam, or were having issues clearing their horses at customs. She chose to go. By the end of the week, it was clear that it would be any hour, any minute then. On Friday night, she slept and did not wake up. Around 3am, I felt a sharp pain in my upper belly and I knew she was gone. I imagined the pain was that akin to the cutting of an umbilical cord that had held us together in this world. I went into her room, brushed her hair, held her in my arms till morning – singing lullabies and songs she had taught me. In the morning, I made the necessary calls then spent the next few weeks in a trance like state going through the motions of funeral meetings, church gatherings, prayers and hymns. I could have sworn that every night in those weeks I heard three men knocking on the roof.

The death of a loved one, kills something in you, but mysteriously still leaves you physically alive – a phantom limb whose loss you will always feel, but never have again.

Chapter 5: King'ori (Njogu and Wambui's son), The Year 2011

My parents were always what I would describe as a happy couple. At least on the outside though. They were the old couple who always gave each other loving looks in church, the couple who always interjected conversations with "My loving wife", "My dear husband". The couple that was always chosen to speak at wedding ceremonies because they had lovely anecdotes of how they had managed to stay together and always painted a rosy picture of marriage. None of those bitter couples who peppered their speeches with "submissive", "compromise" and "not a bed of roses". Paradoxically most people have a twinge of jealousy when they see genuinely happy couples, but it also does inspire hope. It is possible. As such most people had a love-hate relationship with my parents. They envied how perfect their life was, but also aspired to it. My parents had a great role to play in society and I had always known that. They were all actors and they had to play their part really well. People generally stepped out of their roles once they entered the house, but they had to be prepared to quickly put on their masks in case of any impromptu visitors. As such it was highly discouraged to step out of your role for too long. This led to awkward situations whereby my parents would have a heated argument followed by "dear", "darling", "my love", as if nothing had ever happened. I never questioned it. I just took it as a fact of life. Things might not be rosy at home, but no one needed to know that. Stick to the script.

To call my mother overbearing would be a simple way of saying that the English language has failed her by not having a stronger word to really define her. She however was a benevolent dictator, and things only worked in our lives because they had to under her reign. Nothing and nobody wanted to offend Wambui. Everyone was a better version of themselves around my mother as to have been anything else would be a betrayal of her kindness. My mother is kind to a fault – always looking for new causes to support – the children of a drunkard cousin three times removed, a niece in need of an abortion (a fact I found out the day my cousin had a drunken confession) and so on. She is kind, but her kindness is always coated with something thicker – the need to show people how perfect she is and how imperfect they are. Ok, maybe I am being a bit harsh. I lived with her for a long time and that is why I know that she counted acts of goodness and brandished them like a weapon against those who tried to usurp her position as the perfect wife, strong career woman, perfect mother.

Scenario 1: Chama meeting at our house, circa 1993

Mama Chemsto: Praise God! I have great news. Chemsto has been promoted, and has a really big job now at World Bank. I thank you for all your prayers

Mother: God is so good, hee! I remember that time she ran away from high school, and we had to go and plead with the headmaster to let her back in. This is such good news!

Scenario 2: Auntie Chiru's visit, circa 1995

(I eavesdropped on this one)

Auntie Chiru: I need to borrow some money again. Business has not been good, and Muchoki's job (her husband) is not doing too well either

Mother: I will give you the money, but you know I always told you that you should have done a more marketable course in university. You are not good at this business thing

Scenario 3: After church one Sunday, circa 2002

Mother: What is wrong with the church these days? Calling a stupid Mheshimiwa[xii] to the pulpit because he donated one million shillings to the Church? What is one million shillings? [Ruffling through her notebook on good deeds done] Look here! We have given a total of more than five million shillings to the church in the past seven years, and we are on various church committees and host several church meetings in our house. Such ingrates!

Father: Calm down my darling. I will talk to the Pastor and make sure we get a slot on the pulpit this month

Today was one of those days when I really did not need the added pressure of seeing my mother, but we had set a lunch date weeks ago. Things at work were not going too smoothly. I had a really comfortable well-paying job at a high paying NGO (high paying NGO sounds like an oxymoron, but really is not in Kenya). I was the Deputy Chief Accountant with several people reporting to me. Under the national laws we had to be audited annually, and so far we had a clean bill of health. One of our grantors requested an independent audit as they felt the current auditors had a conflict of interest (something about the lead auditor being the son of one of our board members.) The final report was damning. Books had been cooked, and a manhunt was out for this chef. My hands were clean, but as the Deputy Chief Accountant, responsibility fell on me and my supervisor to find the offending branch and pluck it out before it poisoned the entire tree. Discussions were ongoing with the independent auditor to water down some of the findings, but this was proving expensive. Most people could still be bought, but prices were rising these days for whitewashing scandals. We would probably live to get another round of grant funding, but internally we had to get rid of these corrupt elements in our midst who had dared to steal funding earmarked for HIV prevention interventions. Such crimes made me want to believe in Dante's nine circles of hell. Surely, adulterers, tax evaders and people who stole money that was to go to AIDS orphans should not end up in the same hell? It just seemed logical that hell should be really more customized as there were so many ways of being bad, and very limited pathways of being good – One heaven, many hells?

Lunch with my mother was exhausting. She had a way of spotting weakness and attacking when one was weak. A crossbreed between a lioness and a hyena I would say.

"King'ori how are things at work? You look stressed. You know you can always come and work for me and your father."

A valid option, but I would much rather live a penniless existence surviving on porridge and cassava than be back under their yoke, and constantly have to be reminded how much they are doing for me.

"They are good. No complaints. Just feeling a bit unwell. How is dad doing?"

"He is good. The usual – doing too much at his age. You know how your father is. Ha ha! So, are you seeing anyone? When will you make me a grandmother?"

"Ha ha! Not yet mum, I am sure in time it will happen."

"I don't see how you are still single. You are from a good Christian family, good looking, financially stable, well mannered......" stuttering, "Uhhhhhhh, you do like women don't you?"

Laughing, "Yes mum, relax. I like women."

"Ok. You know I have to ask because you know the world has become a very bad place. Do you remember Auntie Rose? The one I used to work with at the Ministry? Yes, the one who always wore that bad wig? Her son studies abroad, and we have been hearing rumors. It is so sad. He grew up in such a staunch Catholic family. The devil really is trying to destroy the sanctity of marriage and family. We prayed against that spirit that is taking over the youth at our last church meeting."

"Ok, mum. I promise I will get a girlfriend soon to put your heart at ease."

The rest of the afternoon was spent at work anxiously going through financial statements to trace the issue. After work, I joined a few colleagues for sushi at a favourite place of ours in Westlands. Regular office gossip ensued spurred on by two of the ladies in the group– Who was sleeping their way to the top? Who was gaining a lot of weight – was she knocked up? Who was due for a promotion? Who was about to be fired? Gossip did not really interest me, but I listened keenly as it was only polite to do so. I think I am an enigma to most of my colleagues. They do not know much of what I do outside work. They know I am not dating anyone, but also have no scandals in the office or outside the office? Two or more female colleagues had pursued me in the past, but had given me up as a lost cause. They could not understand what I was looking for. I was not looking for a sugar mummy[xiii] to supplement my already comfortable lifestyle. I was not looking for a salty mummy[xiv] to feed a void left by an inattentive mother and feed my need to take care of others. I was not looking for a married woman to have a steamy illicit affair with. I was not looking for a single girl to have a fling or a relationship with. I was not looking for a younger woman to help me hold on to a past youth. They probably wrote me off as being asexual and no longer considered me a prospect worth pursuing – which suited me just fine.

After dinner I pretended to leave and go to my Lavington apartment, but in reality I drove to Electric avenue on Westlands to one of my favorite bars. It was a quiet Monday night. I sat up at the bar counter, and the bartender poured me my drink of choice "Three shots of a single malt and some ice." Party music was playing in the background – not really my scene on a Monday night, but perhaps it was a new DJ who was trying to show he was worth his mettle by playing party music when there was no one on the dance floor. Despite myself I started bobbing my head to Davido's "Skelewu." It was hard to ignore the proliferation of Nigerian music in Kenyan clubs these days. It was as if we had collectively as a country given up on coming up with our own authentic sound, and turned to our brothers and sisters in the West who were nothing if not authentic.

Halfway through my drink, I began to smile. Whisky always had that effect on me of making me feel I could get over any hurdle – even the hurdle of close to half a million dollars pilfered right under my nose. A lady walked into the bar, came up and pulled a stool next to me and plopped herself on it. She pulled out her smartphone, "So are you still coming? I wish you had told me sooner! What am I expected to do now? Ah, Whatever!" She hung up the phone, cursed a bit under her breath and pulled out a cigarette from her bag. She was about to light it when she remembered rules had changed. She turned to me and said, "Sorry. I forgot. So many rules these days."

"No worries about that. It happens," I said smiling

I am not one to dwell on my looks, but I have been told that I am a real charmer once I smile. My two dimples appear and it always confuses the ladies.

Her sounding all coquettish and flipping her weave (God, I hate weaves, but she is a looker), "So, what are you doing here all alone on a Monday night? My stupid boyfriend stood me up so I am just going to have one for the road."

"Just having an after work drink, then I am heading home too."

"After work, so where do you work?" This was the part I always hated, the part where a woman was trying to size up your net present value by asking three key questions, "Where do you work?", "Where do you live?" "What car do you drive?" I was probably being unfair to her, but I had been in so many similar situations that I knew where it would lead.

I lied. I made up an average job, an average neighbourhood and she never asked me about my car. The rest of the conversation flowed smoothly with her mostly talking about her boyfriend and me mostly leading her on "Uh huh", "Oh", "That's not good" and so on. Quite quickly I was able to decipher that she was not a gold-digger, and therefore I did not feel I was being toyed around with when I offered to buy her drinks. I am a good old fashioned guy who believes in buying drinks for female company in such circumstances.

A few drinks later, we were both quite tipsy, and she was being quite direct about what she wanted. "You want to come over to my place for another drink" (Why would we leave a bar and go to your house for more drinks, unless we were not really going for drinks?) I was tempted, I admit. It looked like a very clean no-strings-attached plan. I was about to accept the invitation while my usual gnawing fear overcame me. How sure am I there are no strings? This is how men wake up and they are baby daddies or husbands. Do you remember the other crazy one who used to poke holes in condoms? Do you know that you an endangered species – a single man of means in Nairobi? This is how men wake up and they are unhappily married, with six children and more in-laws than anyone would ever care for. What is that Jane Austen line again, "It is a truth universally acknowledged, that a single man in possession of a good fortune, must be in want of a wife." If one let down their guard for a while, you would be unwittingly cured of that want by a Nairobi woman. These streets are mean.

Standing up abruptly I said, "No. Thanks. Sorry. I have an early morning" I fled the scene quickly, leaving more than enough on the counter to cover all our drinks.

I took yet one detour on my way home. It was a road I had been on many a night like this. This was a fact I was not willing to share with anyone. We all have our needs. Down Koinange Street I went. At the sight of my BMW, several half dressed women ran to my car. I rolled down the window and said, "Full night, I want the discounted customer price." My father always taught me to bargain for anything and everything in life. One of the ladies purred, "You are always a good customer, today you get Buy One Get One Free. Me and her" she said pointing to her colleague. It seemed a bit excessive for a

Monday night, but I was never one to turn down a good offer. They jumped into my car and off we sped to Lavington.

I did always find this a much cleaner way of conducting matters of a sexual nature. A fair trade where a willing buyer and willing seller reached a compromise that was optimal for both parties.

Chapter 6: Njogu, The Year 2000

I would like to start off by saying something dramatic such as "it was a cold wintry night", when I first met Nyambura, but there are no cold wintry nights in Nairobi. It was a moderately warm night as most nights are in Nairobi. I was meeting my business accomplice at a certain bar in the city center to discuss our next venture. From some Government connections, he knew about some large land procurements in a certain part of town by foreign investors. While we did not know exactly what they were planning to use the land for, these particular Israeli investors had several successful tourist facilities worldwide and it was our expectation that they would be building something similar in the area. We were buying as many parcels of land as we could off the unsuspecting landowners in the area with the intention of selling it at exorbitant prices once the land in the area appreciated – which it definitely would. It was a certain bar we frequented quite often – good food, cheap drinks and the prostitutes were not too aggressive. One could conduct business in peace. It was also one of the less pretentious pubs in the city center, where one could still enjoy listening to some Congolese soukous music without any fear of the place getting over-run by some big shot Congolese politician and his avid supporters and hanger-ons or some famous Nigerian musician in town and his adoring fans. One of my favourite Mbilia Bel songs, "Nakei Nairobi" was playing when my accomplice walked in.

The waitress who came to our table to serve us drinks instantly caught my eye. I was a regular here and I had not seen her before, but she also had something very familiar about her. I got the feeling that I might have known her from back home in Nyeri. She was cordial, but there was something so withdrawn and fragile about her. She reminded me of a little bird I once found under a tree when I was young. I must have been around five years old or younger. I was playing with some of my siblings outside our hut, under a tree when I spotted the little bird. It was visibly injured and was breathing laboriously. My first instinct was to pick it up and try to help it. My second instinct was to pretend I had not seen it, for it looked as if it would die, and even as a young child I hated getting into situations where I was sure to fail. I turned away from it, and we moved elsewhere to play, but for many weeks after that I always had a nagging feeling that I could have and should have helped it. I had gone back to that spot to look for it the day after I first saw it. It was not there, and I liked to lie to myself that it recovered, regained its strength and had flown off. In reality, it had probably died – its heart beating fast in hopeful anticipation every time it heard footsteps near it – believing someone was coming to save it – then slowing down to a dying diminuendo as it realized that no one was going to save it. Hopefully by the time the vultures got to it, it was actually dead.

Nyambura reminded me of that bird – she was dying – not in a literal way, but a piece of her seemed to have died. Without knowing her, I imagined that she was a girl from upcountry who had come to Nairobi with big dreams. With time and with each new disappointment, she had watched her plans evaporate till all that remained of them was some faint smell in the air – the smell of dreams that had slowly been incinerated over the raging furnace of life's misfortunes. I imagined her misfortunes were probably made worse by the expectations her people back in the village must have had of her. They probably boasted of "our daughter who works in Nairobi" to their neighbours. Those who had been born, raised and would probably die in the village must have looked at her parents with envy, "Look, at the family that has a successful daughter in Nairobi".

I was barely able to pay attention during that business meeting. I kept on trying to catch her eye and when my companion said, "If you want her that much, you can rent a room upstairs," I was filled with disgust that such a thought could cross his mind. Yes, I might not have had the best the marriage track record in the 25 years of marriage I had been in, but for him to have thought of her in that way, tainted the innocence of my thoughts. I shrugged it off and pretended to pay attention the rest of the night.

On the drive home that night, I kept thinking of her. Who was she? Where did she come from? What had she been doing in Nairobi before starting to work at the pub? All I knew about her was that her name was Nyambura (it was on her name badge.) I got into a stupid accident that night as I was letting my thoughts wander as I drove. Some idiot changed lanes on the highway without indicating and as I was not paying attention, I swerved just in the nick of time, but ended up hitting the pavement. The car was slightly damaged and I was a bit shaken, but thankfully I was not injured. As I drove home I resolved to see her again for I knew these thoughts would only get stronger if I did not resolve them.

I spent a dull evening at home with Wambui with each of us pretending to be enjoying each other's company as we usually did. King'ori was studying in a private boarding school out of town, and it was getting harder and harder for Wambui and myself to stand each other's company. For quite a few years, we had turned into roommates who had a child. Love had left our home, taken off in the middle of the night, not bothered to lock the door and had gone in search of a younger idealistic couple – something like what we had been in the beginning – and left us with nothing but a marriage certificate, societal and family responsibilities to hold us together in this loveless union.

The next evening and the few evenings after that I went back to the pub. I sat at the corner each night and ordered the same beer. On the first night she did not show up – I assumed that was her night off. On the second night she was working, but was assigned a different area. On the third night, she was the one serving me. I looked at her face for any sign of recognition and was a bit hurt to realize she did not recognize me. I watched her intently though I tried not to. She was not what I would describe as classically beautiful, but she was interesting to look at. She had a chocolate complexion, big almond eyes that were a bit too close to each other. Her nose was slightly crooked, and seemed to be in constant competition for prominence with her eyes. One could not look at one or the other, but really had to look at both of them to really understand her face. Her most beautiful feature was her lips. They were quite full and seemed unable to fully close. Though I had not even seen her smile once, her second most beautiful feature was her teeth. She had the small gap between her top front teeth that had always been a mark of beauty in a woman in my community. Each feature on her face on its own was not particularly remarkable, but together they elicited curiosity and called for a second look.

At the end of the third night, I tried to start up some small talk when she brought my bill over, but she took one look at my ring and responded to all my questions with a lot of formality. I did not succeed at that point in getting her phone number. I tried to talk to her a few more times, but she was completely disinterested in me.

After a few days of trying and having no luck, I settled on a different strategy.

I got to the bar a few days later, and I sat at my usual place. She came over to serve me and was looking more withdrawn that usual. I asked her in Kikuyu if everything was fine and if there was any way I could make her smile and see her beautiful mwanya[xv] again. Her eyes welled up with tears and I offered her a seat. She told me she could not talk at that time, but if I waited for her shift to end, we could talk. At the end of her shift, we walked over together to a fast food place that opened late and was right next to the bar. I pulled up a chair for her and she broke down almost as soon as she sat down. She blurted, "I was fired! Today was my last shift. What am I going to do? My boss told me it is nothing personal, but that business is not going well and he has to reduce the number of staff. I do not know what I am going to do. Rent is due next week, and I am so broke. I am going to be homeless. Why is all this happening to me?" I offered a listening ear and consoled her as she told me about all her troubles in Nairobi. I was quite right in believing that she had been through a lot of difficulties in Nairobi. She told me about moving here to go to college, about graduating and not being able to find gainful employment, about all the responsibilities she had to her people back in the village and about her absolute feeling of desperation in the city. By the end of the night, I had given her rent money – despite her protestations – and she had given me her number. I promised her that I would help her find a new and better job. This was one broken bird that I was not going to leave to die under a tree and get eaten by vultures. She was my bird.

On my way home, I made a call to my business associate. "Hello, yes this is Njogu....thank you very much....Of course I know I owe you a favor.....A gentleman does not discuss such things.....heeee heeeee. I cannot tell you why I needed you to get her fired. Do not worry though, she will be well taken care of. Yes. Pass my greetings to your wife."

Chapter 7: Nyambura, The Year 2001

Njogu was a godsend. I know it probably sounds wrong to invoke the name of God when I am talking about the married man I am involved with, but he really must have been sent from above. This man met me at such a low point in my life. I had moved to Nairobi and things were going from bad to worse. Although I had graduated from secretarial college, I was not able to get a job. I was almost homeless at many points and the only thing that sustained me were the small amounts of money I was able to get from several odd jobs. I had lived in places that had more cockroaches than people (and trust me, these places had a whole lot of people.)

I met Njogu just in the nick of time. After struggling working odd jobs for a while I had finally secured a permanent position at a relatively upscale bar. While the basic salary was not that great, the tips I made from the wealthy customers were worth all the hassle of working there. Obviously one still had to deal with the annoying customers who believed that working in such an establishment meant I was only one notch above a prostitute. I had my fair share of older potbellied mean men who made lewd remarks and stared at my butt all night, but thankfully the security team at the bar made sure such situations never escalated. I had worked at the bar for close to two months and was beginning to enjoy the little financial security I had gained by being a full-time employee.

I got fired on the same week I met Njogu. It was quite a bizarre week. I had spotted him a few times watching me at the bar, but he seemed harmless enough. He always seemed to be waiting for a dinner date who never quite arrived. I had noticed his wedding band on the first night I served his table, and had been very guarded with him in our interactions. I thought he was attractive for an older man, but as a good Christian, I had never let my thoughts on him wander past a point that would be considered inappropriate. He actually just happened to be there for me at the right time in my life.

One day I went to the bar, and towards the end of my shift I was called into my bosses' office. He was a kind old man, and when he spoke I thought he was about to give me some good news. His demeanor never quite changed whether he was sharing good news or bad news. He told me, "Nyambura, I am so sorry to have to do this to you. I have to let you go. Business is not going as well as I expected it to, and I cannot afford to have an additional person on the staff payroll." I do not recall if I said anything. I was so shocked, and all I could think was "What am I going to do?" I took a few minutes to collect myself then went back outside to finish serving the last guests for the night. I remember looking at all the customers and feeling so miserable. "Look at her – she probably has a car." "Look at him – I am sure he lives in a mansion." "Look at that watch – it could probably cover my rent for a few months." As I was indulging myself in self-pity, my eyes fell upon the one familiar face in the room. The older man who had been here every night this week was at his table. I walked over to serve him, and his first words made me tear up. He spoke to me in Kikuyu asking if I was fine and if there was anything he could do to make me smile again. At that moment, it felt so good to know that in this cruel world, there was still someone who could see me as an individual, as a human being. Everyone else at the bar was probably looking at me, but not really seeing me. I knew that was what happened in a situation such as mine. How many times had I served a table, and come back to collect my bill only to have the people there look at me as if they had never seen me before? In my station in life, I was lucky if people even looked at me, or even acknowledged my presence with a greeting (even if they did not wait for my response.) I took it as a luxury that someone was looking at me, and actually seeing me. Seeing that I was sad. Genuinely asking what he could do to make me happy. We went out later on to a fast food place round the corner, and that is when my affair with Njogu really begun.

It was not what could immediately be termed as an affair. In the beginning I just saw him as a very kind stranger who gave me a shoulder to cry on when I really had no one else to talk to. At the end of our first "date" he gave me rent money, and we exchanged numbers. I knew that it was not a good idea to give a married man my number (or to take cash from him either), but at the moment it felt like divine providence. I was going to be homeless, and an angel was sent to pay my rent. When he called me the next day, I could not ignore his call without seeming ungrateful. That is how it started – with calls and dinners where we mostly discussed how I was feeling, how I was doing and at the end of the night, he probably gave me some cash to help me get through the month. In a few weeks he helped me get a secretarial job at a company that a friend of his managed. Bit by bit we had different discussions and we reached the logical conclusion that it made no sense for him to pay my rent, when he had a huge vacant apartment in an upscale part of town. I felt really grateful to him for all the things he was doing.

As our friendship developed, I got to know much more about him. He told me that he took an interest in me because I reminded him of himself. He told me about his previous life as a taxi driver in Nyeri, about his poor upbringing and about his move to Nairobi with his wife – Wambui. He also told me about the constant loneliness in his life – being surrounded by people, but none who he actually wanted to be with. I could not help but feel really sorry for him when he told me about how his marriage had alienated his family and friends. He told me about how I reminded him of who he was when he started out, and by being with me, he felt he was becoming a better person – the Njogu from Nyeri. With me he could be that Njogu, while with Wambui, he always had to be a refined version of that Njogu – a Njogu who smoked Cohibas, played golf, was a member of all the right clubs, had the "right" friends, spoke the queen's English and liked all other things that wealthy people were expected to like.

On the day I moved into my new apartment, we sat up late talking about life and our hopes and wishes. We talked about a future that included both of us. Up to this point, our relationship had not yet crossed to the next level, but it was as if we both knew that this move to "my" new apartment was the official beginning of our affair. He leaned over and kissed me. The song that was playing in my head at that moment was Dolly Parton's "Don't let me cross over."

I'm tempted my darlin' to steal you away
Don't let me cross over, stay out of my way
'Cause you know that I love you and I'm not the stealin' kind
But I'm faced with heartache here at love's cheating line

Don't let me cross over love's cheating line
You belong to another and can never be mine
I know one step closer would be heaven divine
Don't let me cross over love's cheating line

Moments later as he led me to the bedroom, I knew I was crossing over love's cheating line.

Chapter 8: Wambui, The Year 2005

They did not lie when they said it was not a bed of roses. This is the hardest thing I have ever had to do. Our marriage has survived over 25 years, and it is by nothing other than sheer hard work on my part! You take a man, you upgrade him and then you still have so much drama to deal with. If it isn't the in-laws. Those goddam relatives of his. Such classless people. Does my house look like it was built for people who do not wear shoes? Does my fridge look like it accommodates roots and tubers covered in soil? This is a ladies' place and I will not have riff raff tarnishing its image. To make it worse, his people still resented me after all I did for them. I dug a borehole for them. People in that village used to bathe in the river before I dug the borehole. I even took the jigger eradicating NGO to that area! How can they talk ill of me after all that? Saying "oh, look at the woman our son married, what type of woman cannot give him a child?" "Look how she treats us badly when we go to visit them." "Look how she cannot even cook – what type of woman has a maid cook for her husband?"

His friends were equally repulsive to me. They were a bunch of casual laborers whose people were from the slums or worse still from some interior parts of the countryside. It was such a waste of our good food and drinks when they were around. They drank our good whisky like it was kumi kumi[xvi]. They ate our shrimp like it was roast goat – chewing loudly, swallowing large pieces, loudly spitting out small pieces of the shell. I told Njogu earlier on that he could not expect to get anywhere in life if he was always surrounded by these mechanics, drivers, construction workers, loiterers, vagrants and potential miscreants!

The two things that really doomed our marriage were the other women and the long wait for a child. It was definitely not for lack of trying that we were not getting a child. In the first one to two years we were actually deeply, madly, truly in love and most times could not keep our hands off each other. After that I needed to intentionally commit to biweekly lovemaking sessions even though most times I did not feel up to it. By the third or fourth year, we are at a point of desperation and none of us wanted to discuss the elephant in the room. I believe he secretly resented me for not getting pregnant. He probably blamed it on my use of contraceptives before our marriage. Perhaps he even believed there was something magical I was doing to prevent myself from getting pregnant – maybe some sort of homemade concoctions, some sort of fortnightly coven called together by young, professional wives who were hell-bent on not letting babies wreck their lovely figures or risk their wonderful careers. My pride did not let me tell him how much I really longed for a child, because that would mean us having to discuss why we were unable to get a child. This was a point in Kenya when it was generally assumed that any challenges in conceiving lay solely on the woman. For a society that was modernizing rapidly, we were still tied to our history and culture in so many ways.

In the fifth year of our marriage, lady luck smiled and I conceived. I found out I was expecting a few days after the failed coup in Kenya. The country was still reeling from the hope that suddenly turned into fear and panic in the face of violent retribution that was meted out by the Government. In our home the mood was quite different from the general one in the country. The baby was such a surprise and a blessing for both of us. Initially I avoided letting him know that I thought I was pregnant. I had heard of hysterical pregnancies several times. Perhaps I really was one of those women who so longed for a child that I was making myself throw up, that my period had actually stopped, that my belly was actually getting bigger – not because I was heavy with child, but rather because my hormones were colluding with me to fake a pregnancy. King'ori was such a lovely baby. I know everyone likes to believe that they have the most beautiful baby in the world, but in my case it was true. The fifth and sixth year of our marriage were the best for us. Njogu and I channeled our collective surge of emotions into him. Our previous unhappiness was replaced by unconditional love. We were such doting parents. Though we were both working at the time, we always came home with little gifts for him – cute booties from the supermarket, new rattles and candy. Silence in our house was for a few years replaced with laughter.

One of my favorite memories at the time was going to the Fox Drive Inn with Njogu and King'ori when King'ori was around two years old. They were showing some cartoon about mice, and one particular song that King'ori loved was "There are no cats in America." For the next few months he would keep singing, "Yaaa, no cats in Ameyica, and the yeets a pafe with yeese" (there are no cats in America, and the streets are paved with cheese.) Every time he sung it, my eyes and Njogu's would meet and we would share a look that said, "I think we will make it. This marriage will actually survive."

Unfortunately this joy was short-lived. While we both still loved our son, it was as if we had realized at the same time that did not necessarily mean we loved each other. From the third year of marriage, Njogu had taken to having late night meetings and not always being home in time for dinner. He was in business and business was booming – there was no way I could prove he was not actually having work meetings. However when he came home he always reeked of booze. I had the impression that he intentionally had late night meetings to avoid having to spend time with me once I was home after work. I still believe that he never actually cheated on me until after the seventh year of our marriage. They always say a woman knows such things. Before, his late nights were mostly an avoidance strategy. After King'ori's second birthday his late nights took on a bizarre pattern. Once or twice he came home smelling of booze, but also smelling of a woman's perfume. I approached him about it and we had a major shouting match. I threatened to leave if he was cheating and he lied to me he was not cheating. In either case, we both knew I was not going to leave. The thought of someone leaving their husband for cheating was quite laughable in those days. "Wait, does he beat you? Is he taking care of the bills? Then what is your problem – get back in line and take a number – next aggrieved wife please. Today we are only seeing serious problems – battery and abandonment."

The next time Njogu came home, he came smelling of Cussons bar soap. It was becoming obvious to me that not only was he still cheating, but he was also trying to cover up his tracks, and not be too blatant about it. I felt frustrated and trapped. I needed to talk to someone about it. I obviously could not tell my friends because my life was one they envied or were supposed to envy. If I told them about what was going on in my own house they would feel as if we were similar – them and their drunkards, them and their adulterers, them and their losers. I could not let them think that life was anything but perfect at our home.

I travelled to Nyeri for a weekend to visit my mother. She was always a fountain of wisdom. I poured out my heart to her and she comforted me by telling me that at least he was still coming home to me, at least it did not seem as if any of the women were serious, and at least there was no talk of him taking on an additional wife. For a third wife, my mother had quite a bit of distaste for polygamy. If it was in her hands, I always imagine she would have found a way to get rid of my father's other two wives when he was alive, usurp them and claim her title as his only legal wife. Her parting words were, "Do not start to be a nag. If you nag him, he will not come home. Make the house a place of solace. I think you should also now start cooking his food yourself. Many women have been able to win back their husbands with good home cooked meals."

I did this for the next decade or so and to a great extent I believe the affairs mostly stopped. There was the odd night or two, but for the most part, Njogu was around. We were not happy – far from it, but we got much better at playing a part. We were the couple people envied and we put in quite a bit of collaborative effort to make sure that our public image remained untainted. I also appreciated the fact that there was no public talk of Njogu's affairs and this convinced me further that they had indeed stopped. It would be best for him not to cheat at all, but if God could not grant me that wish, then the second best thing would be for it to be discreet.

Do not get me wrong – I resented him for it. The only problem was that I actually loved him. As such I had to carry this constant burden inside of me because I knew I was never going to leave and I was never going to let him leave me. Not that I ever thought he could leave me. I knew how much he valued the new life he had. All his success and business connections heavily relied on his being with me. He knew that if he sabotaged those, the quality of life he was living would be a thing of the past. I for the most part controlled our joint finances. If he was to leave me, I would do my best to ensure that he only left with the clothes he had on his back when I met him. He knew this too.

One time in 2000 though I began to sense a change. He had been good for a while. All of a sudden he started having several late nights. What filled me with the greatest suspicion was the new spring in his step. He seemed the happiest I had ever seen him in decades. Of course there was the "pretend happy" mode we were always in, but that always disappeared once no one was watching. Before this newfound happiness, we had a very predictable life. In the evenings he read the paper and drunk his whisky while I watched a Mexican telenovela or a Nigerian movie. Communication between us was kept to the bare minimum – updates on what wedding ceremonies we needed to attend, what harambees[xvii] we had to send in donations for, which friends had called and what messages they had passed on. Going through the motions of life, but not really living.

In 2000 he begun to be happy and it worried me that I had nothing to do with his happiness. I decided to do what I did best – I covered up my suspicions. I began to cook his meals myself more often. I began to outdo myself. I began to tell him more often about how much I valued our family and all we had. I began to invoke memories from the past about the day we met, about the day he walked me to my father's door, about the letters we wrote each other, about the songs we danced to at the wedding, the joy we felt when King'ori was born, when he spoke his first words, when he got his first tennis medal. When all these did not work to stop the late nights, I started invoking memories of what he had told me about his difficult upbringing, about how he was struggling when I met him, about how I still accepted him even if he was a poor man's son, about how I got him his first contract, about how he put up his first building with my money, about all the wonderful trips we had taken abroad after his business succeeded. Eventually I believe he came back to his senses, and instead of late nights, I got back my old dear slightly morose husband who sat on his couch in the evenings, reading the newspaper and drinking his whisky. I was thrilled to have him back.

Chapter 9: Wambui's sisters on a call, The Year 2009

Hello, how are you doing?

I'm good, you?

I'm ok. I just heard some news and decided I have to call you immediately we discuss.

Haiya, is everything ok?

It's Wambui.

Oh, God. Is she fine? You are the worst news giver – can you just come out with it!

Actually it's Njogu

Oh, no. What has happened to Njogu?

No, nothing has happened to him.

Then what is the problem?

Actually I hate discussing such things on the phone. I think I should have come to see you in person.

Are you serious? I am already on the call. Out with it!

Ok. A friend of mine believes he is keeping a mistress.

Ok.

That's your only response, "ok."

Well, it is not as if he has always been faithful.

No, this time it's different. I do not mean he has a temporary mistress. It sounds as if he is actually keeping this one. You know – keeping her in a house, probably sending money to her family, maybe even taking goats[xviii] to her family. You know, the full wifing of his mistress.

Uh oh. Ok, this is bad. This friend of yours, can she be trusted? How does she know?

You know this Nairobi of ours is small. She said that the other day she had gone apartment hunting with her daughter. You know the friend I am talking about – the one whose daughter was on the news recently - she is now the head of some Government agency or another. So she is looking to buy an apartment and her mother had gone with her to Kileleshwa apartment hunting.

Ehe?

Then when they were in one of the apartments they went over to the balcony to see the lovely view. When they were there my friend thought she saw a man in the parking lot that looked like Njogu. He was about to get into his car and there was a younger beautiful woman next to him saying goodbye. They exchanged one of those quick pecks on the cheek that might not be that suspicious in other circumstances. My friend has always had a sixth sense so she watched a bit and saw him drive off. She was still not sure if it was him because of the distance, and she also did not recognize his new car.

Uh huh?

So she watched over the balcony and saw the woman walk into one of the apartments on the ground floor. She decided to enquire from the estate agent if any of the ground floor apartments were available and in particular the one she had seen the woman go into to.

Yes...

The estate agent mentioned that the particular one she was interested in might actually be available in a few months as the lady who was renting it, was apparently buying a house in the area and would be moving out soon. She said, "Ah, it must be a big family apartment though, I think I just saw her husband drive off. How many rooms?" The estate agent sneered, but caught himself quickly. "No, it is just a one bed roomed apartment. That is not her husband. She is the second wife of some rich businessman, but he lives with his first wife."

Go on

By this time my friend's suspicions were rising. She is a bit of a busy body, but it has its usefulness at times. So as her and her daughter were driving out, she called the watchman (guard) over and while loosely holding a 200 shillings note in her hand, she told him, "I think I just saw my friend Njogu driving out. Am I right or is my poor eyesight deceiving me?" The guard licked his lips as he looked at the money and said, "I am not sure who you are talking about?" She added another 100 shillings to the 200 shillings and the watchman said, "Ah, yes. Bwana Njogu, the husband of Madame Nyambura. It was him you saw." She thanked him and gave him the money.

This is terrible. Do you think Wambui knows?

Who knows! It is quite terrible, but I do not want to be the one to break the news to her. You know how she is about such things. She will throw a fit then go into denial and then find some way to attack or to hurt the bringer of bad news.

Yes, I know you are right. Do you remember the last time? The time you told her you think you saw Njogu dropping off a prostitute on Koinange street? What did she do? She fired the driver and did not talk to us for almost one year. Then she went round with all her friends discussing our family issues. Talking about how my husband had become an alcoholic after losing his job – which was not true at all. Saying how you were the one keeping your home and how your man does not even bring home milk or bread. You know how such things always backfire on us.

So, what do you think we should do? We cannot just let Njogu run around like that embarrassing her. The least he could do is be discreet about his dalliances. If strangers are already talking about it, it is only a matter of time before she finds out about it.

I think we should keep our ears open and wait to hear more reliable information.

And what do we do if we get the information we are looking for?

Well, it will eventually get back to her. We will have to pretend we never had this conversation. As much as we do not want her to hear the news from strangers, we also need to think about ourselves. Do you want another cold war?

No, not really. You are right. Ok. We never had this discussion. Ok, let us listen out for more information. I will let you know in case I hear anything.

Me too. Ok, greet your people for me.

Excerpt from Capital FM News, September 13th 2013

Kenyan woman has been spared jail for hiring hitmen to kill her husband after the couple promised a magistrate that they had patched up their differences.

The businesswoman walked to freedom after her husband, said he had forgiven her for trying to have him shot in the head and dumped in a ditch.

"I want to forgive her for the sake of our children and family," reports quoted him as telling a Nairobi magistrate. "She is my wife and the mother of my children," he told the court.

The woman was nabbed when she handed Sh40,000 ($450) to undercover policemen as a down payment on the job. Reports said the woman wanted him shot in the head three times, and had promised to pay a further Sh160,000 upon the recovery of her husband's bloodstained clothes and his bank card pin numbers. Detectives said it was her second and possibly third attempt at having her allegedly unfaithful husband eliminated and that an earlier contract flopped when the would-be assassins got cold feet and ran off with the deposit.

The woman's lawyer, said the couple had agreed to patch things up. "The court allows for such negotiations in litigation," he was quoted as saying. "They have sincerely buried the hatchet."

Chapter 10: Nyambura, The Year 2003

Love is indeed a beautiful thing. I never thought I would become the type of woman whose heart skipped a beat every time her man called her. The woman who could be reduced to a state of dizziness by her lover's goodbye kiss. In the past three years of my relationship with Njogu, I had begun to feel that the only moments in my life that were really complete were those when I was with him. 2002 had been a difficult year. It was the year that my mother moved in with me and the year that ended with her dying. Through it all Njogu had been a constant source of strength for me. We saw each other less than was ideal, but whenever we met I was left feeling rejuvenated. Njogu was the true gentleman. Once my mother moved in with me, he insisted on us meeting elsewhere because he did not want to be disrespectful by coming to my home. It was unfortunate that they never got to meet, but he felt it was better that way. "My one regret" he told me after she passed on, "is that I never got to bring goats to her when she was alive and ask for your hand in marriage."

After my mother's passing, I always thought about her words of advice to me. "'Whatever you do, get a child. Please get a child." I did want some form of formal commitment from Njogu before having a child, but I began to realize that this could be a long wait. We had discussed it several times and it seemed very unlikely he would be able to leave Wambui. I was not quite sure exactly what hold she had on him, but there was something, some powerful force or threats that she must have been using to keep him with her. That was one thing I never understood – if both of them were so unhappy together, what was the use of staying together? We also had discussed having him bring goats to my people, but now with my mother's recent passing it put us in a tricky situation. I made up my mind to have a child as I waited for all these other arrangements to come through. When I gave him the news that I was expecting a child, he was beside himself with joy. Him and Wambui had only managed to get one child, and I knew that this gift meant so much to him. It was a really difficult pregnancy with constant morning sickness and high blood pressure. Through it all he came to see me on most days, massaged my feet, rubbed my back and did all else he could to alleviate the constant aches and pains that seemed to be part of pregnancy. I will never forget one day as I sat in the living room with a bucket in front of me (in case I threw up), my feet swollen from oedema, my face all puffed up and covered with pimples. He turned to me and said, "Gachungwa, you are the most beautiful pregnant woman I ever saw." We both burst out laughing because we had no delusions about exactly how I looked, but I appreciated the fact that he always knew the right thing to say to me.

When Njogu Junior was born, I thought I would never know another day of sadness or loneliness in my life. Love for him overwhelmed me and I felt that it was powerful enough to overcome any negativity that life could ever send my way. Within a few weeks of taking him home though, a certain darkness descended upon me. I tried to talk myself out of it. "Nyambura you have such a healthy happy baby, why do you feel like crying?" "Nyambura, you have everything you never thought you would have in life –a lovely baby, a good man, a big house, a big car, a good job, lots of money, more shoes than Imelda Marcos, why are you feeling sorry for yourself? When Njogu was around I would pretend to be fine, but when he left I would fall apart. Njogu Jr. would cry and I would cry even louder. If I tried to soothe him and it did not work out, I started wondering if I was really cut out to be a good mother. Did I really have what it takes to be a super mum? Some women seemed to have it so easy – managing a large house, hordes of children and not skipping a beat. My own sister was one of those women. Six children, a deadbeat husband and she still had time and energy for other people. I had only one child to deal with and a man who while he might not be able to be with me all the time – given his other family and business commitments – still gave me as much attention as he could. Despite all this I was miserable and found myself focusing on what I did not have rather than what I had. My parents were no longer living, I did not have a ring from Njogu, I did not actually have many friends. The one gnawing thought at the back of my mind was that the life I was living was actually not my own. I was trapped in the body of a woman who had plenty but deep inside was a voice saying, "Impostor! You are still Nyambura the barmaid. They all see you for what you really are. You will never belong."

Chapter 11: King'ori and his cousin Wandia, The Year 2011

It had been a while since I had seen my cousin Wandia. We had been quite close before we had both gone to study abroad. She had gone to the US and I had gone to the UK. We moved back to Kenya almost at the same time a few years ago. We kept on bumping into each other at family events, but had not really rekindled our friendship since we moved back. She had called me a few weeks back and we agreed to meet up for drinks on one Friday after work. Today was that Friday. We met up at a pretty rooftop place that was a favourite for many looking for a beautiful place with a good ambience and a lively crowd close to the office parks to the West of the Nairobi city centre. When we walked in, Juliani's new song, "Hela[xix] , hela" was playing. The lyrics were talking about the dangers of placing one's faith in money and other earthly possessions. It seemed strange to have it playing in the background as the crowds clinked champagne glasses. They were having a happy hour buy-one-get-one-free deal and a few drinks later conversation was flowing.

So, Wandia how have you liked Kenya since you moved back?

I think it's ok, but so much has changed. I guess I have changed too.

What makes you say that?

I just remember my first few weeks back – when I was still searching for a job. I would call people up who used to be my friends back in the day and they would promise to call me back to meet up, but they never did. When things started working out for me though is when they all wanted to rekindle our friendships. I don't think that they are necessarily bad people, but I feel that Kenyans have become very economical with their time. A lot of them do not want to see you unless they think you can help them in some way – even if all they get from you is the power of association. "Oh yes! I am good friends with so and so."

That's so surprising. I don't think I noticed that when I moved back.

King'ori you know your situation is different. Your family is Nairobi royalty and has always been. People like to be associated with you even if they do not get any additional perks. Ha! Ha!

Well, I guess you might be right. Just remember though that everyone has their own problems. I might never have to worry about money, but there are always other things keeping me up at night.

Like what? Girls?

You are funny. No, I mean thoughts that keep me up at night.

What is disturbing you?

No, nothing. It is not important.

Hmm. By the way have you met Omosh? He came back from the States a few years ago, and I heard he is doing really well for himself. He got into construction just at the right time. He owns apartments all over the place. I saw him in his Hummer the other day. I always liked him. He is still a humble guy, even with all that wealth.

Yeah. It is becoming hard to find a humble, rich guy these days. Ha! Ha!

That reminds me! Did you hear about John the Baptist?

Who?

John, remember the really religious guy from high school?

Oh, him. John Keter

Yeah. Him. Apparently he used to work in a bank in Michigan, and stole millions through tax fraud. Luckily he escaped before he was caught. He moved back home and is buying up everything. I heard that once a month he has a huge party in different national parks. He owns quite a few park lodges so it is not difficult for him to organize it. People say he has become quite a douche bag though. You cannot say anything about him that paints him in a negative light. He once got his goons to beat up some drunk guy who got mad when John was flirting with his girlfriend. The guy told him, "Who are you pretending to be? We knew you in Michigan when you used to clean poo for a living. Then you stole millions from some bank and now you think you are better than all of us?" I heard they broke one of the guy's legs.

Wow. Ok. That is just wrong.

Yeah, anyway such is life.

...A few drinks later Wandia became a very depressing drunk...

King'ori, do you know I still think about it almost every day? I know my mum and your mum did it to help me, but I still wish I had a chance to make the decision myself. Who knows? I might have also decided at that point too that being a 16 year old mother was going to wreck my future, but I wish I had the chance to make that decision.

I am sorry Wandia. I can only imagine how you feel.

They probably did the right thing. The worst thing was I knew I was pregnant for a while, but I was terrified about what would happen when people found out. I felt ashamed and like I was letting down all the people who had faith in me. I was so ashamed and I kept quiet with the hope that somehow it would disappear. I know it does not make sense. I somehow felt that if I did not talk about it, it would be fine. Some part of me even began to get excited about the life I was carrying inside me. I now know my thoughts were juvenile. I imagined how happy it would make me to know that I had brought someone into this world who would always be mine. My very own baby. Even when I would get to my 90s, I would have this 74 year old child who would be mine. I would never be alone – ever.

Uh huh.

Then one day your mother came to visit my mother. I was extremely nervous – you know your mother is all-knowing. I had not gained much weight and other than general exhaustion, I had no other symptoms that could betray my condition. As soon as I greeted your mother I knew my secret would no longer be a secret. She looked at me quizzically and said, "So you think you are now a woman? You think whoever this friend of yours is will drop out of Form 2, marry you and you will both eat love? Stupid girl! We Maina women do not get pregnant out of wedlock. We have to get this child of sin out of you immediately before you spoil our family name." My mother complied. She has always done whatever your mother tells her to.

I, I am so sorry.

No need to be. I am the one who got pregnant. Anyway, on an unrelated note, when I was in the US I married someone.

What?

Yes. I did. I married him for papers, but he was almost as needy a human being as I am. We fell in love and decided to stay married. I could not tell my family. They would not have approved of him. I just assumed that just like my unborn child this situation would somehow not be discovered. He really loved me.

What happened?

He really wanted a child. I tried to dissuade him. I wasn't sure if I could. The abortion had not been a simple one given the advanced stage I was in when I had it.

So what happened?

I got pregnant, and we were both really excited. Then I lost the baby a few months into the pregnancy.

I am so sorry.

I fell into a deep depression. He tried everything he could to pull me back. We started seeing a therapist who suggested that the best way forward was to try for another child. All the tests showed that I was physically capable of having another child.

So what happened?

I could not face my fear. Two lives had come to being in my womb and had ended before coming into the world. I could not go through another pregnancy, and I did not want to tell him about my fears because I would have to tell him about the abortion.

What did you do?

I decided I had to end it. He was too good for me. I did not deserve him. He deserved someone with less baggage. I am sure I would eventually have hurt him. I decided I had to end it in a way that he would not even think of ever wanting to take me back. I had to hurt him badly to prevent myself from pulling him down this dark path called "my life."

So, what did you do?

I made sure he caught me in bed with one of his friends.

What?

Yeah. Do you want some shots? I think it's time for some tequila. I am beginning to sober up!

Chapter 12: Nyambura, The Year 2012

My heart is bleeding. It has been exactly one week since Njogu last spoke to me. Since I met him 12 years ago, we have spoken at least once every day – even when he has been out of the country. I have seen him at least once a week. Yesterday, Njogu Jr. asked me, "Mummy, why has daddy not come to see us this week?" It killed me. I did not know what to tell him. Some part of me wanted to say, "his other family is trying to keep him away from us," but I knew this would open up a can of worms I was not prepared to open. So instead I told him, "he had to travel, but will come see us as soon as he gets back to Kenya." The first day of his silence I tried calling him a few times – all within the agreed hours of when I could call him – between 10am to 4:30pm every day except Tuesdays and weekends. When he did not pick up my calls, I sent him a few SMSs. At first they were calm, "You must be very busy my love. We can talk whenever you are free." When he did not respond after a few hours, that calmness turned into mild panic, "Is everything fine? You have not responded to my earlier message. Maybe your battery died?" By 4pm, the last SMS I sent him said, "Please let me know you are alive and well. This is very much unlike yourself."

In the evening I still held hopes that he might break our communication time rules and call me at that time. Perhaps some emergency had kept him from contacting me earlier, but now he would get home and see my messages and missed calls and want to put my mind at ease. Around 9pm my phone beeped and I greedily reached out for it. I almost smashed the phone against the wall when I got a spam message reading, "Congratulations! You are the winner of KES 1 Million. To claim your prize please send KES 500 via Mpesa to this number." That night I barely slept. I did not want to sleep too soundly and miss his call. I was sure he would call.

By the next morning, I was sure something was wrong. I broke one of our other rules. I went to his office without notifying him. I did try to notify him, but he was not picking up his phone. I got there and spoke to the guard. The guard knew me and assumed I was a business contact of Njogu's. I enquired if he was in, and was told that he had not yet come in. I asked if he had been in on the previous day, and he said he had. I was getting back into my car to reverse out of the gate when I thought I spotted Njogu's car in the parking lot as the guard was going back in. I ran back to the gate and shouted, "That is his car! He is here." The guard was quickly joined by his colleague. He said, "Madam, I am so sorry. Please do not make me lose my job. We have instructions not to let you in." I pleaded, "Who gave you those instructions! Who?" He replied timidly, "The boss. Madam. Bwana Njogu said not to let you in." I turned back feeling hurt and dejected. I vowed not to cry in front of them. I made it to my car and drove to a nearby street. I parked my car and wailed hysterically. "What have I done to him? Why is he doing this to me? Why did he have to show me such kindness if his plan was then to treat me so cruelly?"

I called in sick to work, went home and cried for hours. Thankfully Njogu Jr. was in school during the day. I cried and texted, cried and texted, cried and texted him in that exact order. I had not received a single response to any of my texts, but that did not stop me from sending any more messages. Maybe, just maybe the next message would be the one he would respond to. Maybe, just maybe this was all a bad dream and I would wake up to a different reality. I went to my pantry and found a big bottle of red wine that he had bought me on his last visit. I took out my laptop and started looking at the thousands of pictures of me and him together. I drank and drank and woke up in a drunken stupor around 5:30pm when Njogu Jr. got home. I warmed him some leftovers and told him I was unwell and would need to sleep early. The alcohol helped me fall asleep but my dreams were painful dreams. I dreamt of myself standing at the top of a hill with Njogu Jr. at the bottom of the hill. He was crying, "Mummy, please come get me!" I tried to get to him but I was surrounded by hyenas. They were gnashing their teeth at me, and I was afraid to move for fear they would attack me. I looked to the bottom of the hill. Njogu appeared as if he was an apparition – almost translucent. I begged him, "Njogu, please save our son. Please carry him to safety." He turned around, ignored me and sauntered off to leave us in destruction.

Chapter 13: Wambui's sisters on a call, The Year 2012

Hello? How are you doing?

I am fine, you?

Not so good. You will not believe the day I have had!

What? Is everything ok?

Are you sitting down? You need to sit down for this.

Ok. What happened?

I have some other bad news.

Clearly. Every time you call me you have bad news.

Ok, just give me a minute. I need to make sure the kids can't hear me.

You know you are horrible at giving bad news. Every time you call with bad news it takes you forever to finally tell me. You couldn't check that the kids were far before you called me?

Ok. I'm back.

Fine.

So, what is the news?

I think I met Njogu's mistress today.

What? Are you sure? What happened?

I am almost positive it was her.

I was in the salon. I had gone in for a hair retouch and a pedicure. You remember I didn't like how they did it my hair at the last place, so I decided to try this new place in Westlands.

Ok.

So, a few minutes after I got in, some mistress looking woman walked in. You know what I mean. There is a certain look. She was extremely elegantly dressed and fully made up at midday – but not in an outfit one would wear to the office. She looked as if she was dressed up for a dinner date at midday. I see those women a lot at the malls during the day – sometimes they are just rich housewives and other times they are mistresses. It is hard to tell who is who, but I have a good eye for detail. The mistresses generally are better dressed than the housewives. I guess one has to be well dressed when you are on the hunt. Us married women do not really have all this pressure. Though maybe we should. If those are the women going after our husbands, we should probably try a little more.

Speak for yourself. I always dress well. Can we have a bit less commentary, and more of the actual story?

Fine! Today you are in some sort of annoying mood. So, anyway this woman walks in and she has come in for a manicure – though her other manicure was still fresh. What a waste. Anyway I guess if someone's husband is taking care of your bills you can afford to get your nails done twice a week. She walks in and she seems to know everyone. She sits and the manicurist starts chatting with her. I wasn't trying to eavesdrop, but it's not as if she was whispering. She seemed to be talking for anyone to hear. No shame at all – these mistresses of these days.

So what were they talking about?

The manicurist is inquiring about her child, and she tells her that he is doing well. Then the manicurist starts poking fun at her about her man. "So, that rich man of yours he seems to be taking care of you very well. " She replies that he is, but that things are not going too well. The manicurist pushes more and the woman starts spilling all the beans. She reveals that the man has a very evil wife – one that he of course has never loved, but one who keeps him to herself using threats. She continues to add that his wife is extremely unstable and always threatens to kill herself if he leaves her. She even says that this wife is with him because of his money and that she trapped him by getting pregnant when they were younger and forcing him to marry her.

Go on.

Of course this time I am eavesdropping only because it is an interesting story, but not because I think it could relate to anyone we know. The more she talks the more emotional she becomes about it all. She starts giving details about how he had promised to bring goats to his people, but she thinks his wife has put him under some evil spell and he is now unable to talk to her. She starts talking about how she is going to take matters into her own hands. "I am moving our son to the school his son from that woman went to. I know they have friends with children in that school. I am also going to start attending their church. That woman cannot think she will marginalize me in this way! Does she know we have a new constitution that gives me the same privileges as her? I am going to fight for my right to his money and property. I am going to fight to get him back from the clutches of that mad woman. I am as much his wife as she is. In fact I am the better one – I make him happy while all she does is stress him." The manicurist comforts her, "Don't worry my friend. Some women are so selfish. Even my man, his other wife was such a problem. She was a nutcase too. I know how you feel."

Ok. I don't understand how this is Njogu's mistress. This man's wife doesn't sound anything like Wambui.

Don't worry. I am still getting to it. The woman starts talking about how she will do whatever she has to do to get him back. She starts talking about how she is even willing to go to the newspapers with her story because she knows that the negative publicity will force his wife to relent. "She thinks she can just sweep me under the rug? I know people in media. She thinks they are the only ones who can be on TV? You know he is a very prominent businessman. He was featured on a business show last week."

It might just be a coincidence. Njogu was not the only businessman featured on that show last week.

That is exactly what I thought, until she said, "You know, people will feel sorry for myself and Njogu Jr. You give a man 10 good years of your life and then he turns his back on you this way."

Oh, God. Did she actually say that? That is not a coincidence.

Yes. I told you that. So I called my friend who spotted her the last time and asked her to describe the woman she saw that day when she was apartment hunting with her daughter. The description fit her perfectly.

Oh, no. Now what do we do?

I think this time we have to tell her. They even have a child! Can you imagine that? He has been keeping this woman for 10 years. To make matters worse, I think the woman is mad. The way she was talking.

We need to warn Wambui so that she is prepared for the drama that will come her way.

This is terrible.

Chapter 14: Njogu, The Year 2012

What have I gotten myself into? A few weeks ago Wambui found out about Nyambura. I knew that I would not be able to get away with it forever, but I never knew how bad Wambui's reaction would be. It was not as if we have been a happy couple. I think what set her off was finding out that this has been going on for a long time. The realization that I have been committed and dedicated to someone else for over a decade. It was all my fault she found out. Once you carry on an affair for so long and go undiscovered you begin to feel invincible. I began to get sloppy – late nights at Nyambura's, dinner and drinks in less clandestine restaurants. I think someone must have mentioned something to her that got her suspicious. One Saturday I forgot my phone at home. By the time I got back she had gone through all my messages.

I came home later in the day unaware of the fight that awaited me. She was standing in the living room with her arms akimbo. "So you take me for a fool? You think you can have your cake and eat it? Who is this Nyambura bitch who you text every day?" I was surprised because Nyambura's name was saved as "Cement grinders, Mombasa" on my phone. She continued, "Oh, you think I am stupid. I read all the messages on your phone very carefully. The ones to this number were the most dubious. I called the network provider and through some contacts of mine I was able to get the name the number is registered under. What do you have to say for yourself?" I had been caught with my pants down and I must have tried to stutter out some excuse, "No. It's not what you think. I can explain." She pushed me to start explaining. That was the point I realized I actually could not explain. She was shaking in anger. "So you think you can just go running around town with this woman? You did not even have the decency to be discreet? I have to keep hearing from people that you are being seen in different places with this woman? Njogu, you know I made you and I can break you. I am telling you now to break up with this woman and never talk to her again. If I so much as hear you have seen her again, I am going to go to the cops with the documents I have from that 1988 land deal. You know I have enough information on your shady dealings to put you in jail for life. Corruption is being taken very seriously these days!" I knew she was not bluffing, and there was no way in hell I was going to let her disclose the information she had. My days in Nairobi would be numbered if those details ever emerged – even if I was fortunate enough to not spend the rest of my days in jail.

I cut off Nyambura. It was for her own good as much as it was for mine. Wambui is a formidable enemy and one who would crush Nyambura without a moment's thought. I had to endure weeks of the silent treatment in the house. I always wondered why Wambui fought so hard to keep what we had – because what we had was a terrible marriage. In a few weeks I began to believe that Wambui was warming up to me again, but that was quickly changed one day after her sisters visited her. Wambui was livid, "How could you! How could you!" I kept on repeating that I was sorry about the affair. She added, "You even have a child with her? Have you no shame? Do you know what type of mess you have gotten us into? You were going to take goats to her family? Have you no respect for me?" She broke down crying and I tried to comfort her as I wondered how she had found out all this additional information. I had not thought she would dig deeper about Nyambura once I had ended it all. I had assumed she wanted to know as little as possible about it considering she was still going to stay with me. Why would she want to torture herself with all these details? Women!

I think the devil got into Wambui that day. She started saying, "We need to get rid of her! I cannot let her come out in public with this. We are going to eliminate her." I thought a good night's sleep would get her out of this delirious state so I prepared her a cup of warm chocolate. She fell asleep. At 2am she came and found me asleep on the couch. She switched on the lights and said we had to talk. She had hatched an elaborate plan to get rid of Nyambura. She laid out the plan and a cold chill ran down my spine at the deviousness of it all. She planned to fake her death and frame Nyambura for it. Her last words that evening were, "You will follow through with this plan. You are the one who got us into this mess and you will help in getting us out. This woman cannot destroy the life and the image I have built in all these years of hard work!"

Her resolve got stronger once the text messages from Nyambura started coming to her. I had a knack for picking the crazy women. The one crazy woman who was sending messages to my wife about "becoming co-wives" and "living in harmony together like the biblical Sarah and Hagar before the rift" while the other crazy woman was plotting to fake her death in less than a month and have the other crazy woman be blamed for it. I did the best I could to convince Wambui not to carry through her plan, but given my precarious position in all this, I knew when to sit back and let fate have her way.

A few words of wisdom from the wise

Have you ever heard that old kikuyu folk tale of the hyena and the crow? Which one you ask? Heee, no wonder this new generation is lost. How can you know where you are going if you do not remember your past, your history, your culture? Anyway, I will tell you the story – that you might tell it to your children and your children to their children after them.

One day, the hyena and his friend the crow were taking a walk. You ask why a bird was taking a walk? Silly question! Just know I said they were taking a walk. It was a cloudy day, but not a cold one. Hyena looked up at the sky to see if it was going to rain. His eyes fell on the clouds, and all of a sudden his belly began to ache. He had not realized how hungry he was. The more he looked at the clouds, the more his belly ached with hunger. In time he began to realize that the clouds bore an uncanny resemblance to delicious fatty meat. Before his very own eyes, the clouds turned into delicious piles of fatty meat. Crow inquired, "My friend, what are you looking at so hard that you almost tripped over that stone." Hyena responded, "Look! Up at the clouds. Do you see that?" Crow replied, "What? The clouds?" Hyena replied, "No, stupid. Fatty meat." Crow responded, "Oh. That."'

With some imploring, hyena was able to convince crow to fly with him up to the skies to enjoy the fatty meat. They flew and flew and flew. In time, hyena began to see the meat fat getting closer. He was salivating. The rumbling in his tummy grew even louder. Saliva dripped from the side of his mouth. He began to smell what must have been the fatty meat. Began to think about its wonderful texture. The amazing taste it would have as it went down his throat and as bits of the fat melted and dripped from the side of his mouth.

He closed his eyes and he was able to imagine the wonderful taste of the fat in his mouth.

Crow shook his body vigorously. Hyena panicked, “ey, man. What do you think you are doing?” Crow did not relent. He shook and shook until the feather hyena was holding on to fell off. As hyena, fell, rapidly approaching the ground, the last thing he heard from Crow was, “goodbye.”

Moral of the story: Who knows! Maybe something about bad shit happening for no good reason? At least we now know why the hyena’s back legs are shorter than the front ones and why the hyena limps.

Chapter 15: Nyambura's sister, The Year 2013

I do not know how Nyambura got herself into all this mess. It is such a shame. I always told her that in this life we should be content with the little we are given. My sister's problem is that she was always an ambitious one. But you see where such ambition lands you? In jail! In jail for life. Of course I know Nyambura has been framed. She could never harm a fly, but what was she thinking interfering with these rich and powerful types? When she had Njogu Jr of course there was no more denying she was messing around with someone's husband. It was obvious – we never met the man, then all the money she suddenly had. It does not take a genius to figure out that she was being kept by a married man named Njogu. It really was such a damn shame that she named her son after him. Why are people wasting names[xx] these days? If a man has not married you, the least you can do is name your children after your own parents.

When I first heard that Nyambura was being tried for murder, I was terrified but hopeful that the truth would eventually come out. When details emerged about whose murder she was being tried for, we all gave up hope. There are certain people who are above the law and Wambui Njogu and her family were clearly some of these people. Nyambura could have had her pick of many men, but instead she chose to go after one of Nairobi's most powerful women's husband? It is sad though that this woman had to die under such mysterious circumstances, but it is a well-known fact that she had many enemies. Any of them could have killed her and realized that framing Njogu's mistress would be easy. The most damning thing was when they found Wambui's bloodied clothes buried in Nyambura's garden. Not even the best of lawyers could exonerate her from this situation. That was the first nail on her case's coffin.

It really hurt Nyambura to see Njogu testify that day in court, "It is true, Nyambura had become violent in the past years. I believe she has been losing her mind. She also did threaten to harm my wife and that is one of the reasons I had to end our affair. I am not saying that she killed Wambui. I do not believe she could resort to such measures, but I am saying that it cannot be completely ruled out." Nyambura was sitted next to her lawyer looking like a rabid dog. Her appearance definitely did not make the case for her innocence any stronger. What I saw in front of me was a broken and betrayed woman. Her hair was rough, her outfit was mismatched and oversized. In the few months since she had been arrested she had lost quite a bit of weight. Her nails that were usually perfectly manicured, were broken and ragged. Her eyes were red from crying herself to sleep every night. The whole combination made her look deranged. When Njogu finished testifying, she jumped up and ran towards him. Before the court policemen could grab her, she began to wail, "Liar! Liar! How can you do this to me? How can you – the father of my child – come to court and lie like this? What have I done to you? What have I done to you to deserve this? This pain is too much! Please hang me! Please hang me! Hang me for I am already dead now!"

She was pulled away from Njogu before she could do any harm, but the eyes of everyone in the court seemed to say the same thing. "Guilty. This woman is definitely guilty. Did you see her just now?"

She was sentenced to life in Langata Women's prison. I took in Njogu Jr., and got to keep a few of her personal possessions. Most of the property was taken back by Njogu and his goons. Can you imagine even the logbook for her car was in his name? She walked into prison, the same way she came to Nairobi – with nothing else but her name.

Chapter 16: Nyambura, The Year 2012

None of them understand. They think I lost my mind. What they will never understand is that Njogu will always love me. He has always loved me. Someone must have poisoned his mind for him to wrong me like he did, but I know he will come to his senses and get me out of this prison. All our problems started early last year when he started avoiding me. I know it must have killed him. I am sure Wambui made him do it – she realized that I was getting more powerful than her in this relationship of ours. I tried all I can do to reach him but to no avail. I will not be surprised if she bewitched him – maybe went and got some herbs from a witchdoctor and brainwashed him.

I write him letters almost every day. I think they must be hiding the letters he writes back. It is all so confusing – the murder case and his silence for close to a year before that. I have not yet figured it all out, but I am sure that he has done this for our own good. I refuse to believe he would betray me. Perhaps, someone was threatening to kill me and his only way to keep me safe was to have me locked up. I know that any day now, he will walk in to rescue me. He will come as my knight in shining armor – steal me away by night, and take me to a land where we will only know happiness. A world devoid of pain and suffering. One where our love will no longer be illicit. A world where my son can have a father. A place where no one will look down upon me as "a husband snatcher" or "that barmaid."

I think he has gone to that place to prepare it for me. It must be the reason why he has not come to visit me in jail. He is very busy in the preparations for our life after prison. It is unfortunate that Wambui is dead, but perhaps this was the best way. We could not have shared him forever. I do not like to speak ill of the dead, but she was the main problem in our relationship. She could not be happy with what she had, she wanted to have all of Njogu – even if she knew I was the one keeping him happy. She was like that woman in King Solomon's story. There was a disagreement between two women with both of them claiming to be the mother of a child. King Solomon ruled that the only fair way to deal with the situation was to cut the baby in half with a sword and give each mother half of the child. The child's true mother exclaimed and begged for the child to be left alive and given to the other woman, while the false mother was in agreement with cutting the baby into two. Wambui reminded me of that false mother. She would rather have Njogu be unhappy and incomplete, but have a piece of him with her.

I think they are trying to poison me here in the prison. There is a conspiracy to eliminate me before Njogu comes to rescue me. I can see it in the other women's faces. They whisper as they pass me on the corridors. They all look at me strangely during our dressmaking classes. I have never been good at making friends, but I am not even trying to make any friends here. One cannot trust these people here. They are hardened criminals – some killed, some robbed others – maybe even at gunpoint, some smothered their babies in their sleep, some evaded taxes while others colluded with tax evaders. Really a group of untrustworthy individuals. I am going to eat only as much as I need to survive until Njogu comes to rescue me. I cannot let him come and find me dead. I cannot imagine how heartbroken that would make him.

Prison life is not easy – especially for those women here who know they will be here forever. No one is on their way to rescue them. There is one woman who walks around every day singing church hymns loudly. I overheard the other women during lunch saying she used to be a televangelist whose fame was rising faster than those who had set up her megachurch. They framed her for fraud and that is how she ended up here. Apparently she still has a huge following outside, and the prison cannot let her followers visit her because they are quite fanatical and cause chaos in the prison speaking tongues and singing inflammatory hymns about "Joshua fought the battle of Jericho, and the walls came-a-tumbling down." It is not good to give prisoners hope about walls that can tumble down. Since the televangelist is no longer allowed to have visitors, she leads her own services in the garden when she can. I once joined in but when I realized the hymns were all hymns of the persecuted, it left me feeling even sadder than I was when I joined. "Am I a soldier on the cross?", "Down at the cross," and "By the rivers of Babylon" did little to lift my spirits.

There are also the other prisoners who are embittered. There was a particular woman whose main refrain was "You know I learnt who my real friends are when I ended up here. All those people on the outside just loved me for my money, my beauty and whatever else they could get from me. Do you know only two people ever visit me now? My house help and a friend I had in high school. Just the two of them. No one else wants to be associated with a criminal, though they were always happy to reap the benefits of my crimes." She is not particularly beautiful so I always wonder what she is referring to when she says, "they only loved me for my beauty."

The other types of prisoners were those who were still in denial about their situation, and thus held some form of elusive hope. "I am innocent! It will be found out soon. Just wait." "This is a temporary situation. They made a mistake. I should be leaving here any time now. You can give me your letters to take to your loved ones. I am sure I won't be here more than another week."

The last type of prisoner was the one who had come to terms with their situation, and had nothing to look forward to. These were usually the most dangerous as they felt they had nothing to lose. They were the ones who could sometimes be found starting fights with prisoners or threatening wardens. "I am going to be here till I die. What do I have to live for? My children will be raised by strangers. My family will soon forget me. It would be better if I had been shot dead or hanged."

The day the policemen came to get me from my home I was terrified. I was sleeping when I heard a bit of commotion at my gates and heard the guards let in someone. I immediately assumed it was thieves and hid in my wardrobe. I heard the loud footsteps as they budged into the house, breaking all my locks in an instant. I knew that the burglar alarm would go off any minute and was safe in my belief that in a few minutes the security team would arrive and catch the bewildered thieves. The burglar alarm went off, but it did not seem to stop the intruders advance into the home. I could hear them flinging doors open looking for something. Finally they opened my bedroom door and shouted, "Police! We are looking for Nyambura!" I did not budge. It was the oldest trick in the book – criminals pretending to be police. In a few more minutes, I heard the security squad storm in. From my little peephole in the wardrobe I was able to see them confront the criminals. Rather than the showdown I was expecting, there were some polite salutes exchanged, some documents shared and finally one more authoritative call for me. "Nyambura Kimani, you are under arrest." A sob escaped my lips and this helped them locate where I was. I was given a few minutes to dress up and then taken to the police station in handcuffs.

At the police station, I sat on a rickety bench as my fingerprints were taken. Everyone was looking at me like a wanted criminal. Not as a suspect, but as a wanted criminal. Finally a policeman came in to begin my interrogation.

Where were you six days ago on the morning of Wednesday 28th March 2012?

I..I....I can't remember

Well, we will just have to throw you in jail then won't we?

No, please give me a minute. I am confused. What day is today?

3rd April 2012! Are you telling me you don't remember where you were last Wednesday?

Ok. Please one minute. Wednesday I was at home all day

Can anyone else confirm you were at home on that day?

Err, err. No. Maybe my son. He was picked by the school bus at 7am in the morning and left me at home

What time did he get back home?

Err. The school bus dropped him back home around 6pm

So, there is no one who can confirm you were at home all day?

Inspector, please I I I need to think clearly

I am not an Inspector! I am a Senior Superintendent!

I..I am sorry.

Why were you at home on a Wednesday. Do you not work?

I do, but that day someone told me to wait for them at the house

Ah, so you do have an alibi. Who is this person and what time did they come?

Ah, actually, they did not come. I waited all day, but he told me that he got held up and could not make it in time.

So you do not have an alibi?

No, I do. I can show you my phone. Please, please look at that. You will see that I was waiting in the house for them.

(Out of desperation I pulled out my phone, and started scrambling for the SMS. I handed the phone over to him).

He read out loud with a mocking voice, *"My darling gachungwa. I know things have not been the same between us for a while. I want to come by tomorrow and explain everything to you. I will come to your home. I will confirm to you the time when I will drop by tomorrow."*

Madam Nyambura, this does not count as evidence. You want me to believe that based on this one SMS you did not go to work, and quite coincidentally this person did not show up?

No, Senior Superintendent, you have to understand that this is a very important person, and we had not spoken in a long time.

Who is he to you?

He is the father of my child.

What is his name?

He is Njogu Njoka of Njogu Enterprises

Ah. Now this is making more sense. So you decided to kill his wife because you are his mistress. I see how you think madam

What? What?

Yes, Madam. You are under arrest for the murder of Wambui Njogu who went missing last Wednesday morning. She left home for work early that morning and was never seen after that. From investigations with her family and friends, almost everyone has identified you as a prime suspect. We are going to have to hold you until we can get more evidence on the case.

I fainted.

Chapter 17: Muriungi (Nyambura's brother), The Year 2012

Loneliness is a strange thing to bring up with anyone. If you are lonely, yet you are surrounded by people they think that you are saying that they somehow cannot provide you what you really need. If you are lonely, yet alone, you dread coming off as needy. Imagine meeting a stranger and telling them, "I am lonely." The first thoughts in their mind will be "Oh no! This person will be a problem. They will be a leech. Stick to me and bleed me dry. "I therefore chose the next logical path. I decided to be wilfully lonely – at least that way it seemed I chose loneliness – rather than the other way around – loneliness chose me.

I remember the first time I realized I was bound to live a life of solitude. I was young. It was a weekend. The neighbours' children had come to visit us. I was with both my sisters – Nyambura and Mumbi. In total there were seven of us – the three of us and the neighbours' four children. We were playing with marbles. At some point I stood up to stretch my legs. I walked around for five minutes. When I came back I stood and watched all of them. Conversation flowed as if I had never left. No one noticed my presence in the sidelines. That was the first moment I realized that it did not matter if I was with people or not – either way I sank into the shadows. I was bound to be alone even if I was going to be surrounded with others. I was bound to be forgettable even when I was in the midst of those who loved me and those I loved. I was destined to be lonely whether I was alone or with others.

I cannot tell exactly when I made the decision to be a wanderer. One day I stood up and made the decision to no longer be invisible but rather unavailable. Maybe it was destiny or perhaps it was my name. I was born to be the Wanderer who never settled down anywhere.

I have seen a lot. I have made the journey from Nairobi to Cape town. I have traveled from Nairobi to Algiers, crossed all the paths from Nairobi to Dakar. In all those years, I have learnt one thing – people want you more when they believe someone else wants you or loves you. I have told women in Bulawayo, "No. I can't do this. I have to think of my family in Nairobi," and I have seen them instantly care for me a bit more. The fact that someone else cared for me or loved me was enough to make them believe I was worthy of that too. One woman in Lagos tried to convince me to leave my imaginary wife. "She cannot love you as much as I love you. Please do not leave me. Why do you have to go for Cotonou?" Do you imagine that you will find greater love there?"

When I came back to Nairobi a few months after Nyambura's arrest, I was petrified. I knew so little about my sister's life, but to come back home and find out that she was in such a terrible situation. That just galled me. I went to visit her in jail exactly once. I tried to comfort her as best as I could. I told her, "You deserve better than this. I am so sorry." She replied, "I really appreciate the support I am getting from friends and family." I looked deep into her eyes and realized she had no idea who I really was. I had just confirmed I was invisible.

I left the day after for Lilongwe. At least there I might find some people who cared for me – even if they only cared for the illusion of me.

Chapter 18: Wambui, The Year 2013

It is 3am and he still has not come home. I would have settled for the same kind of unhappiness we had before I faked my death, but this new unhappiness is something I cannot bear. I realize now that my expectations of what would happen after my return were unrealistic. I have eliminated Nyambura and I thought that was all was needed to restore the happiness I thought we once had. I now realize that we were unhappy long before Nyambura came into the picture. Njogu's indiscretions were a symptom of a major illness rather than the condition itself. While the festering wound of his adultery was what stood out the most, this marriage was rotting long before all that. We have been held together by nothing other than our mutual unhappiness, and my undying love for this man who I hate almost as much as I love.

Dark thoughts overpower me these days. One of the hardest things is that I cannot form any relationships with my friends and family again. As such I am all alone in the world except for Njogu. He is my everything right now because I have nothing else. The other day King'ori came to visit Njogu. Visit might not actually be the right word for it – he came over to give him a piece of his mind. I knew that the two of us should not meet. I was not sure I could manage to keep my identity hidden with him – a mother's love and affection is difficult to mask. He did not know I was in the house, but I heard their heated argument.

Dad, you could not even wait for mum's soul to be at peace before getting another woman?

Don't you dare talk to your father like this! How can you raise your voice like this? Do you have no respect for me?

Oh, so I can't talk about it even though everyone else is talking about it? You know they are all wondering what type of man gets a new woman after his wife is murdered by his mistress. You are the reason she is dead! Your mistress killed her! Dad, do you hear me? Your mistress murdered my mother.

Do you think I am not suffering? Do you think this has been easy for me?

Oh, poor you. Look at you suffering. Poor you! Poor dad, with his mistress in jail! Poor dad. You do not deserve any of this. You played no role in it!

Don't dare raise your voice! I am your father!

Yes, that you are! The father who got my mother killed.

Shut up! You are being hysterical. You don't know what you are saying.

I know exactly what I am saying. How do I even know you didn't get mum killed yourself? You know they are all saying that she is the one who controlled all the money in this house. They are saying you might have hired someone to kill her and then framed your mistress. They are saying you are a monster!

Son, don't listen to them. They don't know what they are saying.

Of course. I should trust you, right? You who kept a mistress for all those years. You even have another son! How can I trust anything that comes out of your mouth?

King'ori, you are upset and have had too much to drink. You don't know what you are saying. Let me get my driver to drop you home.

We can talk about this tomorrow morning when you are in a more stable frame of mind.

Oh, so now you are saying I am unstable. Well, let me tell you something dad. If I am unstable it is only because I have grown up in this shitty unstable home. Don't you think you two had already messed me up enough growing up? Now, on top of all that I am the person people whisper about. "Look at him. Poor guy, do you know his father killed his mother?" "Do you know his mother's body has never been found, but the father's mistress was arrested for his mother's murder?" "That guy's family is so messed up. I don't even know how he is functional after all he has seen."

Don't you dare curse in this home! You must be losing your mind. You are going home now and we will talk about this tomorrow.

You think you are still the one making decisions? Mark my words, dad. This is the last time you will see me. The next time I will see you is when you are dead – and that will only be as a courtesy. I don't think anyone else would bother themselves to organize your funeral. It is the only favor I will owe you as your first born son – hoping I am actually your first born son. For all I know you could have more bastards running around town!

--

That night Njogu was inconsolable. I tried to comfort him and assure him that King'ori did not actually hate him, but was just in a bad state of mind. I could tell he resented me even more than ever. He probably blamed me for all that had happened, and wanted to forget the role he played in all of this. What I had done was to fix a situation that he had gotten us into.

Since that day he has been coming home even later than before. He stumbles in always after midnight, almost always extremely drunk, stumbling through the door and barely making it to the couch. He has not slept in the bed for weeks. Sometimes he does not even make it to the couch. He just passes out wherever his legs lead him to. It is so embarrassing. No one visits the house anymore, but I see the look the cleaning lady sometimes gives me. It is a look of pity. I am that creature who is now pitied instead of envied.

I think he detests me. I have had a lot of time alone with my thoughts when he is away. I have lived a long life, but when I replay it in my mind the key highlights seem to be the unhappy life we have had together. Sometimes really briefly I see a flash of my younger days – a carefree existence full of hopes and dreams. I see myself in my campus dorm with my girlfriends, enjoying our newfound freedom in Nairobi. The next place memory lane takes me to is meeting Njogu in Nyeri and the excitement of true love. After that I see myself in my wedding dress at a wedding full of more observers and naysayers than loved ones. A wedding of people coming to confirm that I was actually marrying a driver. The next stop in memory lane is the resentment of his relatives and the first few years of marriage when my thoughts were always punctuated by the loneliness of not having a child. Then there is the sad memory of losing my father – he died of old age, but sometimes we like to think that those we love will be with us forever. After that there is a happy memory of King'ori's birth and the glimpse of happiness that came with his birth and his early childhood. The next memories are those of the years when I thought Njogu was cheating on me. The ultimate climax of this tragedy was finding out about Nyambura and her son. That was the ultimate betrayal, especially the realization that this was not a fling, but rather that he had been having another family for over a decade. Of course life has had its joys too – my career, success, close friendships, wealth and more. However my unhappiness with Njogu seems to have overshadowed any other joy I found in life. It has been the stained paper on which the rest of my life has been written on.

Sometimes I think of ending it all. What type of life is this I am living? One where the only companion I have in the world loathes me. I stay up all night waiting for a man who does not even come to sleep in our bed. I try to cheer up a man who probably blames me for all his misery. I am a good Christian though. As much as I despair, I cannot opt out of this life. I must survive! This marriage must survive. He was in love once. I am sure with enough effort I can remind him what that felt like. There was a time when we made each other happy. A time he was my world and I was his. I will keep cooking – even if he chooses to eat out. I will keep asking him how his day was, how everyone else is doing – even if he does not respond. I will keep trying.

Chapter 19: Njogu, The Year 2013

I hate this life. I cannot believe Wambui dragged me into all of this. What type of evil monster did I marry? I cannot blame her for hating Nyambura, but to frame her for murder? Then to blackmail me into colluding with her? In my few moments of sobriety these days I see the look on Nyambura's face that last day in court. The look of hurt as I betrayed her. She did not realize she was just a pawn in Wambui's evil plot. I wish I could unlove Nyambura. I wish I could unmeet her. I brought her into this mess. That day in court I thought I would confess to all. I never actually thought I would be able to utter all the lies Wambui had told me to. I lacked courage though. I wanted to save Nyambura, but when I realized saving her would mean damning myself, I chose the easier option. When I had to choose between myself and the one I love, I chose myself. I kept thinking of what society would say of me when they found out how I had joined Wambui in this elaborate plot to frame my mistress for her murder. I also thought of how I would definitely spend the rest of my life in jail if Wambui revealed the business secrets she had promised to reveal if I did not follow through with her plan. I knew that if I did not follow through with Wambui's plan, I would be a damned man. My life, my wealth, my family, my businesses – I would lose them all. Now I realized I am still a damned man – I sold my soul when I sent an innocent woman to jail to save my skin. I sent the woman I love to rot in jail for the rest of her life. I sent the mother of my child to jail because I am a weak man. A man who while he despises the life he lives now, immensely dreads going back to the life he had before. A life where he had nothing.

What do I have now? My own son hates me. He has vowed to only see me once I am dead. What kind of curse is this? People see me and pretend they have not seen me. Who wants to be associated with such an unfortunate man? A man whose mistress killed his wife.

I have thought about going to visit Nyambura in jail, but I cannot bring myself to it. I do not know what I would tell her. An apology would be meaningless, unless I was getting her out of jail. I cannot stand to have her look at me and see what a weak meaningless creature I am. This is worse than the time in my childhood when I left the wounded bird on the ground. This time, I took the wounded bird in, nursed it to health, then broke its neck just as it thought everything was fine. I am a cursed man. I have nothing to gain in this life. I deserve this misery.

Chapter 20: King'ori, The Year 2013

I woke up in a cold sweat the other day. The strangest thing about nightmares is that once you explain them to someone else they never sound quite as scary as they were when you had them. When you were having the nightmare though you were terrified, even if it was something as mundane as a red eyed teddy bear chasing you with a lollipop. This nightmare left me terrified. I woke up at 4am and I fought any urge to go back to bed. I knew it was one of those nightmares that would continue where I left off as soon as I closed my eyes. In the dream I was lost in a deep dark forest. I was trying to run somewhere- perhaps to safety. My legs were moving faster than I ever thought they could, but when I looked at them I realized I was not moving at all. It was as if I was on a treadmill – no matter how fast I ran, I did not move anywhere. I started hearing noises in the forest. At first I thought the sound was that of howling dogs. As the sound got closer, I realized it was closer to a laugh than a howl. For a moment I wondered what type of people were in the forest laughing in the middle of the night. As the voices drew closer I realized that it was not a human laugh, but the laugh of hyenas. I tried to move, but all I could do was run in place. I was panting, when I saw the pack of over 20 hyenas. They laughed, that insane laugh of hyenas. They drew closer and closer. I could see their fangs, see the saliva dripping down their mouths. Suddenly they morphed from hyenas to humans. I recognized a few faces – that of my kindergarten teacher, that of my parents' gardener, their house help, my boss and a few other faces that were familiar, but not immediately recognizable. Their laughs were evil and changed from laughter to screaming. It sounded like what I imagine a wailing banshee would sound like. They crowded in and I fought harder to run, but could not move. I woke up in a cold sweat.

I lay awake in bed until it was time to get ready for work. I wondered about the significance of that nightmare. Did it have something to do with the turmoil in my life since my mother's murder? Did it have something to do with the investigations that were still taking place at my workplace since the disappearance of the money? Did it have something to do with the fallout with my father? The whispers in the office about what was going on with my family? The "friends" who no longer returned my call. I was under a lot of pressure these days. It was a miracle I could even fall asleep with all the thoughts running through my mind.

I got ready to go to work. On arriving I greeted the guard and he gave me a look of pity. I was beginning to get these looks almost everywhere I went these days. The whole court case had garnered a lot of media attention and everyone now knew the intricate details of my family's life. I drove into the parking lot, parked my car and got out to walk to the entrance. On my way I bumped into the Finance Director. I waved at him and he pretended not to see. He got to the door before me, swiped his card and quickly got in. I thought his behavior was strange, but he was always a strange man. I got to the door, swiped my card and it did not work. I tried swiping it again but to no avail. I thought that perhaps my card was faulty. I walked to the guard to tell him I needed him to let me in. The Managing Director drove in just as we were speaking. The guard faltered in his speech and the MD seemed to understand what was going on. He got out of his car and said, "Sorry about this. I did not want it to happen this way. Please wait in the guard's cubicle. I will be back in a minute." I still did not understand what was going on. A few minutes later the Finance Director came out with a box and a letter. He handed them to me with a somber look on his face, and said, "The letter will make things clear. Have a good day." He then walked away. I was baffled. I quickly opened the letter and it read as follows:

Dear Mr. King'ori Njogu,

This is official communication about your employment termination. The recently concluded investigations point to you as the only culprit behind the missing funds. We have notified all our donors and other partners for them to immediately stop any communication with you. We have decided not to seek legal redress against you for the sake of the negative publicity it will bring to you and to the organization. We ask you to respect these wishes and to accept the generous severance package enclosed. If you do however seek to take legal action, we wish to assure you that we will spare no resources to make sure our good name is not tarnished.

Sincerely,

The Human Resources Manager

I was dumbfounded. I immediately hoped that this was some form of elaborate joke and that at any moment someone would burst out laughing and say it was all a prank. Nothing of that sort happened. I looked up and saw a few familiar faces looking at me through a ground floor office window. As soon as I looked at them they all pretended to be going about their business. In that brief moment before they looked away I saw various emotions. Some were of pity, while the majority were of disdain and disgust. I walked to my car as stoically as I could. I had had enough of this public humiliation.

I got into my car and started driving to nowhere in particular. After a few minutes I pulled over in a small shopping center. I opened the box and inside were all the personal things I had in the office – my lucky mug, an extra tie, a stress ball, a few accounting books and a pack of chewing gum. I decided I needed a drink. I walked into a nondescript bar in the shopping center. I ordered a bottle of whisky, but to my disappointment it was too early for them to serve alcohol. I had forgotten about the new alcohol laws that prevented the sale of alcohol before 10am. I sat down and had a cup of ginger tea, as many questions ran through my mind? Who had backstabbed me? How could the organization inform everyone else about firing me before actually firing me? Even the guard knew! Who else had been told about this? Was I now a pariah in the NGO world?

As I was sitting, sipping tea, swatting flies away from my table and feeling sorry for myself, I received a text message. It was from one of my female colleagues called Moraa. The message read, "We need to talk. Meet me at noon – the usual place in Westlands." I knew it was going to be a discussion about what had led to my dismissal. I needed to know how all of this had transpired. I stayed at the bar I was at and had another cup or two of tea before 10am. At 10am I finally got my bottle of whisky. By the time I was leaving for Westlands at around 11:30am I was very drunk. I drove as carefully as I could with the Nairobi sun beating down on me and making me feel extremely dizzy. At every roundabout, my heart skipped a beat as the policemen did their usual random search of insurance sticker's validity in traffic. I was extremely nervous because all they needed to do was ask me a question to realize I was drunk. I finally got to Westlands a few minutes before noon.

I walked into the bar and found Moraa sitting on a bar stool drinking a Smirnoff black ice. She was not much of a drinker so I knew she really must be on edge to be drinking so early in the day on a work day. We chose to sit at the back of the bar where it was quite deserted and we could speak freely.

I ordered a bottle of coke and a glass of ice. I had sneaked into the bar the remaining half bottle of whisky I had bought at the other bar. Without my job I was going to have to learn to cut costs. No need buying more alcohol at this bar when I already had my other bottle. I discreetly poured myself a drink and Moraa started talking.

King'ori I am so sorry for you. This shit is just too much. Please tell me you won't tell anyone we met and talked today? I hate this place, but you know I have my 2 year old daughter to take care of alone. I cannot lose this job.

No worries. I don't even know who I would tell. You were the only person I was close to at work.

Ok. I don't even know where to start. I want you to know though that I only found out about all this today – or rather I only found out you were the chosen scapegoat today. Otherwise I would have told you earlier.

Ok. Please tell me. I really want to know everything. This is all stressing me out.

So, on Friday I heard that the investigation was complete and that they had found out who had stolen all the money. I didn't know who it was, but I had my own suspicions. Then today in the office I came in and heard you had been fired. I was so shocked. I knew you were being framed. I was in the office kitchen warming some tea when the tea girl started confiding in me. She was talking about how shocked she was that you had been fired. Then she whispered to me, "You know the bosses were here yesterday – on a Sunday. That must have been when they had the meeting to discuss firing him." I asked her how she knew that and she said that she found dirty dishes in the Grants Director's (Lomunyak's) office. I decided there and then I was going to talk to him about that meeting. You remember I used to sleep with him back in the day? He owes me some favors. Actually now that we no longer work together I can tell you he is my daughter's father. This stays between you and me by the way. His wife doesn't know.

Ok. So what happened?

I went to his office and told him I knew there was a Director's meeting that had happened yesterday, and I bluffed that I knew some of the details. You know the Directors don't trust each other so he had no reason to doubt me.

What did he say?

He is not a bad person, and he has always liked you. He just started confessing about everything that had happened.

And what is it that happened?

The report that came out on Friday proved that it was the Finance Director who stole all the money. He did not deny it when he was called in on Friday. He said though that he had stolen it to support his father's election campaign last year. Now you know his father became the Governor of his county. The problem is that since then his father has signed a Memorandum of Understanding with our organization to get us preferred registration status in his county. When the deal is finalized, we could be the largest recipients of HIV funding in that county given our close relationship and support from the Governor and our links to donors. I think his son started up this partnership agreement because once the investigations began he realized he would be discovered and needed to find a way to become indispensable.

Are you telling me I have been framed because the thief has the right connections? This is so unfair.

Yes. On Friday when he was approached that is exactly what he told them. He told them that if they chose to terminate him, all those favors would go away with him and he would ensure that our organization never gets to work in his father's county. The Director's meeting was arranged to discuss what to do about the situation. Lomunyak says that at the Sunday meeting they decided they had to get a scapegoat. The donors want to see someone get fired and penalized for the theft, but the Directors know that they need the Finance Director too much.

So how did they decide I was to be the one to go?

They realized that you were the only other person senior enough in the Finance Department to have access to the accounts. The negative publicity your family has been having this past year also played a role. They felt it would be easy for all to believe that you also have a secret life. Most of the people in the office have no ill feelings towards you, but you also don't have many close friends there. You were an easy target.

Is there anything I can do?

No, I am sorry, but it appears they have covered all their bases. In the words of Lomunyak, "the donors want to know that whoever was responsible for this heinous crime, will never find another job in Nairobi."

We ordered another round of drinks and the song playing in the background was coincidentally Muthoni the Drummer Queen's "Nai ni ya nani?"[xxi]

Chapter 21: Njoroge (Wambui and Njogu's Mr-Fix-It), The Year 2013

I am a man holding a very expensive secret. I have always been the man who holds expensive secrets, but this particular one is one I deserve to be paid for. I have been an errand boy for Wambui for too long. I remember last year when I brought her the package containing her new identification documents. She did not even give me a word of thanks. She just handed over the KES 100,000 balance as if what I was doing was a normal type of job. Sometimes I even wonder if she even knows my last name. You work for someone for close to thirty years and realize that they might not even know your last name or even where you live. That is how these people are. They are so used to having everything and knowing that they can get anything they need from the rest of us at whatever price suits them. We need them and therefore we accept their mistreatment for a few pennies, and the assurance of food in our bellies.

I called Njogu and told him I urgently needed to talk to him. I assured him I had some information for him that would be extremely valuable. I left my little shack in Kibera Laini Saba. I got into a Number 8 matatu[xxii]. Thoughts ran through my mind as the matatu drove. From Kibera we got onto Ngong road. I looked at the new skyscrapers coming up on the road, the several malls, and the new apartments. I wondered who decided that some people should have access to all these wonderful things while the rest of humanity is left to wallow in poverty. I began to think of Njogu – what made him so different from me that he should have all he has while I had the little I had. Our villages were close to each other. He also had as little education as I had. In fact I think I had a year or two more of schooling than he did. I did not think he was any more hardworking than I was. So by what merit was he to have a huge selection of cars to drive to our meeting while I was here squeezed in this matatu with more and more passengers filling in? With people so tightly packed into the matatu that only a portion of one's buttocks were firmly placed on the seat with the rest levitating above the seat and a part on your neighbors thigh? What had Njogu done to deserve the type of life he lived and what had I done to deserve mine?

As the matatu sped down Ngong road, I watched all the people in their private cars, comfortably sitting. Some drivers and passengers taking a minute or two to look at their smartphones – obviously on some sort of social media. The main concerns on their minds must have been about how bad the traffic was – no real problems for this lucky lot. As we passed the largest Government referral hospital, I felt so annoyed that I had only been to Government hospitals. Of course I was in no way wishing to be sick, but I heard such marvelous stories about people who went to private hospitals. Some hospitals that were better than any hotel I had ever been to. Hospitals where you had your own doctor, and never had to line up on long queues to be seen. Apparently there were even some hospitals where the nurses were friendly and where hospital staff smiled at people. Oh, the lifestyles of the wealthy.

Finally we got into town and on Haile Selassie Avenue, I looked at all the Nairobi women. People who were in skirts so short and heels so high that they surely must have driven into town. There is no way they could have come in public transportation in those outfits. I saw people in coffee houses sipping on coffee and eating delicious delights. I looked at the skyscrapers flanking both sides of the avenue, and wondered who owned these buildings. How did they get the money to make such buildings? Where were they born? What did they eat? Where did their children go to school?

Finally I got off the matatu at Railways bus station. People were pushing to get into the matatu as I was pushing to get out. Finally I tumbled out of the matatu with my coat almost ripped due to the commotion at the matatu door. I tripped into a puddle of mud, but caught myself before I fell face flat into it. A mkokoteni[xxiii] zoomed past me almost hitting me. On the back of it were tens of sacks of potatoes and one of its operators lying on top of the sack of potatoes taking a nap in the midday sun. Human traffic was everywhere making it very hard to get to my destination. A man with a solitary can of some deadly looking cockroach poison bellowed loudly in Kiswahili, "Cockroach killer! Cockroach killer! 50 shillings! Kills your cockroaches and your neighbour's cockroaches! The cockroaches will never even think of coming back after how they will see their comrades die!" A woman wearing a large skirt, worn out sneakers, a shawl and a head scarf approached me and said, "Excuse me? I am lost. Can you please help me?" I ignored her and quickly crossed the road. One could not trust such strangers anymore in the streets of Nairobi. Too many bad things had happened to would be good Samaritans – getting drugged, being put under some sorts of evil spells, finding themselves withdrawing their life savings at a bank and handing them over to complete strangers with no recollection afterwards of how they found themselves in such situations.

I walked down Moi Avenue to the café we had agreed to meet at. Njogu was already there by the time I walked in. He looked quite unkempt and his eyes were red either from lack of sleep or too much alcohol.

So, Njoroge. What is it you wanted to talk to me about?

Let us wait to order food first. "Ng'aragu ndihoyaguo uhoro." You don't start discussions with a hungry person.

After we had eaten, I started the conversation.

Njogu, I have some information that you will find quite useful.

Ok, what is it?

Before I tell you, you have to promise me that I will be rewarded well for this expensive information I am giving you

Well, it all depends on what the information is

I can assure you that it will be worth quite a bit of money. I want only one assurance for the information I am giving you.

What is that?

You will give me one of your newest cars in exchange for the information. I only want one of the cars you bought after 2011

Well, that can be arranged but as I said, it all depends on the type of information you are giving me.

I can assure you that it will be worth it.

Ok, then tell me.

I know Wambui has been missing and is presumed dead as of last year. What you might not know is that she is actually not dead. She faked her death to frame your mistress. I got her documents to allow her to escape to Dubai.

Ha! You are a funny man. You think I did not know that? Since you were in on it, I can even tell you more. I know about you getting her the documents. I know about you burying the bloody clothes in Nyambura's garden.

You...You..You were involved in all this? H..H...How? I thought she was doing it to punish you and your mistress?

It is a long story. I am not even sure why I am telling you this, but she is even back in the country. We are together again. Of course given your role in all of this, I do not see you going to tell the police anything. Well, so is that all you had for me? You can clearly see that your information is not worth a car, let alone even 1000 shillings. Are you done because I am ready to leave.

Wait! Wait! I have something else for you that will be worth a car and maybe even more.

Well, I doubt it but go ahead.

I narrated to him a story from close to 30 years ago that I had never ever told anyone. At first he doubted my story, but the more I went on, the more he realized that I was saying the truth. The details I provided were more than enough proof that what I was saying was true. It felt strange to open up as I did. In fact some would have considered it foolish of me to share information such as this that could backfire on me. Once he realized I was telling the truth, he became extremely mad. His violence could have easily turned on me, but the Njogu I had in front of me was a broken man. An hour into the conversation I was able to convince him that I was not the enemy, but rather Wambui was our common enemy.

We walked over to a bar nearby. The news I had given him needed to be washed down with many drinks. The more we drank, the more his anger towards Wambui grew. I could see him hatching a plan in the silent moments of our conversation. A few hours later he spat out, "That evil bitch! To think of what she has taken me through. To think that she made me abandon Nyambura my love, and put her in jail and have to hear the agonizing stories of how she is going mad. To think of how she always acted like she was the pillar of virtue in society, and treated me like I was the problem in our marriage. All the threats and blackmail she has used to keep up this sham of a marriage we have had for all these decades. Do you know I can count the number of times I have been truly happy since I married Wambui. Most of my happy memories in our marriage do not even include her. She was all that was wrong with my life. I think I was even happier when I was a poor driver. At least those days there were people I knew I could trust. What do I have now? Everything a man is expected to be happy to have, and none of the happiness that it is meant to bring me. I have no family. I have no friends. You know you are probably the closest friend I have at this time, and you are not even my friend. I am telling you all this because these are the thoughts I have locked up in my mind and no one I can share them with. You know she always wants to win! Even in this situation, she has won. I have lost Nyambura, I have lost the love of King'ori! He hates me. He wonders what type of father I am – the type who would get a new woman less than a year after his wife was murdered. Now with this news, I have also lost the trust I had in Nyambura. What type of life is this? What type of life is it where a man cannot even trust those closest to him?"

After a while, he said with quiet resolve, "I will give you my newest car. You just need to do one last thing for me."

We deliberated and agreed that the terms were fair. I was happy to help him in this final assignment.

Chapter 22: King'ori and his cousin Wandia on the phone, The Year 2013

King'ori, why is your picture in the newspaper?

Er, I don't know what you are talking about?

Page 23 of The Daily Nation. I am looking at it right now. The caption reads, "The person shown above is no longer allowed to conduct any business on behalf of Acme Health Partners." Why is your picture in the papers? Almost half the page is taken up by your picture. What did you do for them to do this to you?

Wandia, I really cannot talk about it now. This is not a good time.

When is a better time then, huh? You have not returned any of my calls since your mother's burial last year. King'ori, we are all really worried about you. I have come to your place a few times, but the guards always tell me you aren't home. I called your father the other day, and he told me you two haven't talked in months. Then to see this today in the newspaper! What is going on with you. I am genuinely concerned.

Wandia a lot is going on in my life and I am just not ready to talk about it. Maybe in a few months, but I don't want to talk now.

Can I at least come see you this week? I know you are free now that it is clear you have lost your job.

Let me let you know.

King'ori I don't think you will call me back. It has taken me a long time to get you on the phone, I want you to commit to a date when I can visit you.

It's complicated. I moved out a few weeks back.

That's fine. I can understand directions. Where do you live now.

Wandia, I am really not in a good situation to talk right now.

King'ori do you think I have not heard the rumors? They are calling you a drunkard. They are saying you are in debt – that your car was repossessed and no one even knows where you live. Why don't you just pick up your father's calls? He can help you. You know, you can even move in with me if times are that hard. I don't believe what they are saying about you having stolen millions from Acme. I know you are not that type of person. Go back to your father. He will help you get back on your feet. This is just a passing cloud. We can all help you get through this.

My father is dead to me! I don't want to hear anything about him! Do you know all the things he has done? Do you know just what type of man he is? You all see him laughing, smiling and cracking jokes , and you think you know him. He is worse than the devil. He is dead to me! You hear me! He is dead!

Please don't say that. I don't want you to be cursed. You think my mother is not upset by how things have turned out? Your mother was her sister. None of them is happy about the situation. You have to remember though that he is still your father. You have to respect him for that. I don't want you to get cursed for what you are saying.

Well, isn't it too late for that. I believe I am already cursed. There must be a reason I am going through all this.

Please, my dear cousin, listen to me. We want to help. I can even come by now. Please tell me where you are. I know you are in a bar. I can hear the noises in the background.

I really do not want to talk. I have to go.

Please don't hang up on me. I don't know when I will be able to find you again. Please, please King'ori, hear me out. I want to help. King'ori? King'ori? Hello? Hello? Are you still there? Oh God.

Chapter 23: Nyambura, The Year 2013

Last night I heard the three men knocking on the roof. I awoke suddenly around 2am and asked my cellmate, "Do you hear that? The three men on the roof?" She looked at me in anger at been woken up at that hour, and turned over to continue sleeping. I took the knocking as a good sign that freedom was about to come my way. No one knows it yet, but I am going to leave this prison soon. How can they expect me to stay here for life? Do they know I have Njogu and Njogu Jr. waiting for me on the outside. I have a plan.

I am eating very little here. I want to get so emaciated that they will have to send me to a proper hospital. When they do that, it will only be a matter of time before Njogu comes to get me out. If he does not come to rescue me as soon as I expect, I am sure I can also manage to escape from the hospital. I am sure I will not be guarded as closely there as I am guarded here. It is a tricky balance though. I have to eat just enough to survive, but not too little that I actually die.

I have had a lot of time to think things through in prison. Time is the one thing in abundant supply when you lack freedom. All the time in the world, but no ability to do the things you wish you could do with that time. I now know that Wambui was the problem all along. If she had never been in the picture, Njogu and I would have been extremely happy. It is now my mission to get out of here so that Njogu and I can start out afresh. I know we will have a chance of happiness now that Wambui is out of the picture.

I have thought of it many times. The three of us living in a huge house in Karen – obviously not the same house that he and Wambui lived in – that would be odd. The three of us living as father, mother and child – an idyllic scene. The three of us going to church together on Sundays, and having people look on with envy, "Look at her beautiful hat!", "Did you see that car? How many CC do you think it is?", "Did you see their bodyguards? These are some very important people." Obviously we would have to also go to a different church than the one him and Wambui used to go to. People would gossip too much if we moved around in the same circles. Of course there would be some awkward moments and some disapproving looks from judgmental women, but it would all be worth it. I would be Njogu's official wife.

My partial hunger strike sometimes gets me disoriented. I start remembering things that never happened. I begin to doubt Njogu's loyalty to me – I start to worry that he might have found someone else on the outside. I start to think that perhaps prison is all a terrible nightmare and that I will soon wake up. Then I tell myself that in times of difficulty – such as these times – my faith in those I love should not waver.

Chapter 24: Wambui's cleaning lady, The Year 2013

This stupid man! You do so much for a man and what does he do to you? He decides to bring some old woman from Dubai to act as his wife. I even started cooking matumbo for him! Does anyone know how much matumbo stinks? It stinks! I cook, I clean, I take care of him as only a real woman can, and he decides to get another woman.

Sometimes I wonder why I have even worked in this home for so long. I am the one constant in Njogu's life and he has never ever appreciated me. His wife was very cruel to him when she was alive. She always treated him the way she treated the rest of us servants. "Njogu, do this. Njogu do that." Then his other mistress. I don't even know what to say about her. She killed the Madam of this house. Who does that? The way our system works is that no one should get greedy. We can all share – isn't there enough money to go around? Njogu always knew how to take care of me. He always gave me a bit of extra money after our afternoons together. He would say, "Go buy your children something nice," or "go cook some meat for your husband tonight." I always felt that he understood me and the types of troubles I had back home. I could tell he was not always this rich. He was a rich man with a poor man's manners. I could tell how much Wambui resented him for his past. Whenever her childhood friends were around she always tried to cover up for him or embarrass him – depending on whether they were on good terms or had recently fought.

The things I have seen in this house! I should even have been asked to testify in court. I started working for them almost immediately after King'ori was born. I was initially meant to move in and live in the servants' quarters but I think they had one major fight where it was decided that I should come to the house almost every day to work, but never live in the same compound. I later found out from Njogu that Wambui had trust issues and was worried about having another woman live in the compound. So much for that. He started coming home in the afternoon almost two weeks after I started working for them. I have done this job for a long time. I know how to keep a job – no need to tell the madam about things she doesn't need to know about. His first few drop-ins were quite innocent. He would pretend he had forgotten something at home. A few days later he started getting bolder. He told me exactly what he wanted. I started cleaning up the house faster in the mornings so we could have our hour or two together in the afternoons.

I once had a scare. After one of our afternoons together, my panties went missing. I searched everywhere, but could not find it. He had already left to go back to work and I had to search alone. I looked under the bed. I looked in between the sheets. I took out all the beddings and shook them but to no avail. I looked under the pillow, the rug, the carpet, but it could not be found. I was terrified. I knew that soon Wambui would be home and I would have to vacate her room. I prepared dinner and waited for her to get home. She released me early in the evening. I went home and wondered how I was going to break the news to my husband that I would be losing my job. I was sure that if Wambui found those panties, I would be immediately dismissed. She might not even know I was the one involved, but she would know that I had been keeping secrets from her. Later in the evening I got a text message from Njogu. It was in Kikuyu and read, "I hope you are not looking for your panties. I took them with me so that I always have a part of you with me." I smiled to myself then instantly got mad at myself. This stupid man will get me fired! I need to stop feeling for him whatever I am feeling.

The best year of my life was definitely the year after Wambui was killed. Njogu was a broken man. His mistress was in jail and his wife was dead. This was my opportunity. We spent most of our afternoons in bed together. He kept on telling me, "I am not a good man. Do not fall in love with me." I kept on thinking to myself, "Neither is my husband. At least you are rich." I took care of him and nursed him back to life. He was extremely distraught after Wambui's disappearance and the whole court case. That one year gave me so much hope. I knew he could not survive for long on his own. I was already playing the role of a wife. It was only a matter of time before he asked me to move in. Of course it would be a bit sad to leave my husband. One does not stay married for over 20 years without having some sort of affection for the person they are married to. My children would probably also be upset but I was sure that they would be happier once they knew their school fees would always be paid.

One morning I came in to the house and I knew something was different. I could sense another woman's presence in the house. I opened the door and found some woman's shoes at the entrance. I walked into the kitchen and the strong smell of matumbo almost made me throw up. He must have forgotten to put it in the fridge once it cooled down. I walked over to the stove, and started packing the food. I waited for him to come meet me as he always did every time I got into the house. He came out of his room and brought this woman with him. I was annoyed, but I did my best to conceal my anger. "Good morning. Meet my friend Peris. She will be staying with us for a while. She just came back to Nairobi from Dubai." I smiled politely and greeted the woman, and tried to block the voices in my head that were saying, "I told you! You were not good enough. He was always going to get a woman in his social position. You are only good enough for him to sleep with, but not good enough for him to marry."

This new woman has really destroyed the life I thought I would have with Njogu. She never leaves the house so these days we have to go see each other at a lodging. He noticed I was upset the first time we met up and he told me, "My gachungwa. You know you are the only one for me. This is a temporary situation." I believe though that I am the only one he really cares for. I just cannot wait for this Peris woman to go back to Dubai or wherever she came from.

Chapter 25: Wambui, The Year 2012

They always say that one can never really know the things that go on behind the closed doors of a marriage, except for the two in the marriage.

I was not going to have any of it! For this foolish mistress to think she was going to take from me, everything that I worked so hard for. What annoys me the most is the secret knowledge I have – knowing that her child with Njogu is not actually Njogu's – but not being able to tell anyone about it. It is the one secret that by revealing I will slowly start to unravel the life I have built in the past decades. Nyambura's baseless claims on my wealth are all built on the grounds of her having a son with my husband – an untruth that only her and I know.

The first years of our marriage were difficult ones – financially we were doing well, but tensions between both our worlds started to emerge. As hard as I tried, I could not get his family to see me as anything other than as a wealthy woman who was expected to save Njogu's whole family from poverty. I did the best I could, but I felt a sense of resentment from his family. They needed me, but they resented what they perceived to be an attitude of superiority to them. I did my Christian duty of being a good wife and good daughter in law, but when that did not endear me to them, I decided to cut them off. The last straw for me was when they began to say cruel things about me when we still had no child, close to five years into the marriage. They began to say that I was "a man", "a cursed woman who was denying their son a child" and in either case, "a woman who would make a horrible mother." I tried not to let them get to me, but it was really hard in a society such as ours that values a woman most for her role as a wife and a mother.

One weekend in 1983 I went back to Nyeri to visit my mother and confided in her about the situation I was in, and the toll it was taking on our marriage and on my happiness. She told me the following story:

"My child, there was a time in our history when our tribe did not believe that a man could be incapable of fathering a child. Any time a couple could not conceive, blame was solely placed on the woman. Women being the smart creatures we are, learnt that we had to find our own solutions to such problems in a way that saved face for the men. Society allowed such women to discreetly have affairs solely for the reason of getting pregnant. It was always kept secret, but most men knew when they were incapable of having children. Even if they suspected their wife was sleeping with another man to bear children, he turned a blind eye to it because he knew it was saving his dignity – and that she was doing it for both of them – to keep their family together. Do you know why my co-wives loathe me? They knew that I was your father's favourite when he was alive, but the real reason they loathe me is because they do not believe you and your sisters are his actual children. People ask how he could have had children at that old age. Wambui, deep in his heart, your father knew that he could not possibly have fathered children at that age, but he also loved me and respected me for giving him that illusion – one that let him believe he was strong and virile even when he knew that he was withering away. In your situation, maybe you are the one with the problem, but there is only one way for you to really find out. Do not sleep on your ears and ignore what I am telling you my child."

I heeded her advice and made a suitably discreet arrangement of my own. 10 months later I gave birth to a bouncing baby boy – we named him King'ori.

They always say that one can never really know the things that go on behind the closed doors of a marriage, except for the two in the marriage. I believe that even some of the things that happened behind the closed doors of a marriage are known by two or three – some of whom are not even necessarily in the marriage, while the other partner can be quite oblivious to some of these happenings.

I know that Njogu is infertile, but for me to come forth with this information – will not only damn Nyambura, but also myself.

Chapter 26: Njoroge (Wambui and Njogu's Mr-Fix-It), The Year 2013

I am going back home to Kibera Laini Saba after my night out with Njogu. We stayed out all night, and it is the early morning hours as I go back home. It has been raining hard, and it is quite a task to get to the matatu without getting drenched. I cannot help but smile all the way home. Soon, I will have my very own car. I am very pleased as I think of how once I have the car, I will pass pedestrians and splash water on them! Let them know that I have a car, and that we are not on the same level. I think of how with my big car, I will be able to look down on others who are driving small cars – maybe even frighten them a bit at roundabouts. Oh, you think you have the right of way? Well, let's see how brave you are once you see my big car.

I think of all the women who I will be able to attract with that car. I should have no problem getting a second or even third wife. All it will take is one or two trips to my rural home, and I will be able to come back to Nairobi with a new wife. I will be a big man in my area – the man with the big car that jumps over portholes. My car will always be clean and shiny. People will look at me in traffic and wonder who I am. "That must be a wealthy businessman," they will say. Or, "He must be some important political figure. Did you see the car he drives?" I get home and find my wife making breakfast. She is at the small paraffin stove making our morning tea. She gives me a dirty look as I walk into the house at 6:30am. I pull up my favourite plastic seat and plop myself on it. She begins her usual fight, "All you know how to do is drink! When will you get a real job? When I married you, you lied to my family you were a big man in Nairobi. It has been 20 years and we are still here living in the slums. You need to stop all this foolishness. Why are you always working with rich people and never getting rich yourself?"

She continues to complain in the background, but my mind is only occupied by one thought – I am getting a car.

Chapter 27: Wambui and Njogu told by the narrator, The Year 2013

Njogu got home and found Wambui in the kitchen. Wambui greeted him and he responded as cheerfully as he could.

I am good. How are you?

I am fine. I have been waiting for you to come home. How was your day?

It was fine. Yours?

It was good. I made you your favorite meal. Ugali and matumbo.

Thanks. That is wonderful. Should we go to the dining room?

Yes, we should. Give me one minute. Njogu, now that you are home early I need to talk and get some things off my chest.

Tell me what is on your mind?

I just wanted to tell you that I know we have been through some hard times but I also know we have known some happiness. I have been thinking a lot with all this free time I have had. Do you remember our first dance at the wedding?

Yes. I do. It was to Waigwa Wachira's "Marry me."

You are right. That has been the song playing through my mind. I just wanted to let you know that I really loved you, and still do even though I know now that this is ending.

What do you mean it is ending?

Let me speak. I have a lot on my mind. This is it. This is the moment I have been dreading for so long. It is the moment I have faced so much sadness to avoid. I need to end it all. I don't really know where to start. Sad thoughts have been filling my mind for the past few weeks – sitting alone in this house with only my thoughts to keep me company. I have mulled over this decision. I have thought this over for countless days. I have prayed for God to show me the right way. I have cried and cried and wondered how I will ever get the strength to do what I must.

What are you trying to say?

It is over. I am tired. Tired of you. Tired of us. Tired of arguing. It is time I moved on with my life. With my new identity I should be able to start all over again and forgive myself for all I have borne. Holding on to this dead thing has made me resent you. I do not hate you, though I know I should. I resent myself for all these decades of lying for you – covering up for you, making excuses for you. I love you and somewhere deep inside of you I believe you once loved me.

You know I have always loved you.

No, don't say that. You don't need to lie to me anymore. You may love me, but this is not the way I want to be loved. It is killing me to leave you, but if I stay I may as well consider myself dead. The truth has been staring me in the face for so long, but I was afraid to let go of you. I wondered what society would say about me. I have wondered countless times how I could live without you. I have just realized that for the past few decades I have not been living, merely existing. I have seen my smile move from being a real smile to one that is only on my lips.

Don't say such things.

It is the truth. I have been a perfect wife to you and more. I have loved you, supported you, given you my body and my love. Yet you have never found that to be enough. I pray that no one ever makes you feel the way I have felt. No one deserves to go through this. I am done with lying for you and covering up for you! My heart has been bleeding for too long.

You! You think your heart has been bleeding? Do you know what I have been through?

I don't care what you have been through? You have deserved all the problems you have had. So what? Your mistress is in jail! Do you think I care? Did I tell you to get a mistress?

You really have no heart! You sent an innocent woman to jail to pay for a crime she did not commit.

Do you think I care! Did she feel sorry for me when she was destroying our marriage? That woman was going to ruin us! I don't know how you could have been that stupid!

You are such an evil woman! Don't you realize I loved her! She was the one good thing that happened to me during our marriage. She did not deserve all of this.

Well, you brought her into this. Didn't you!

I love how you act as if you are the most virtuous person in this country. Do not for one moment think you are devoid of sin.

I might not be a saint, but compared to you, I could be one.

Oh. If that is the case then I must be imagining what Njoroge told me!

Wha...Wha...What did Njoroge tell you?

Oh, so now you want to know. You are testing me? I know everything that transpired between the two of you.

My love. I do not know what you are talking about. I just want you to know that everything I have done, I have done for you.

Yes, I am sure that is what you told yourself as you slept with Njoroge!

No! No! No! You need to understand. I did it for you. We tried for so many years. I knew you really wanted a child.

So you decided to sleep with our errand man?

No! Please don't raise your voice. You just don't understand it. I had to! You know our marriage was falling apart. We needed a child.

And you decided to sleep with Njoroge.

You know we tried. You cannot have children! It is not my fault. I did not want you to be shamed. I did this to save your dignity.

How did you save my dignity? I have been raising two children who are not mine?

My dear. Please do not look so upset. Please stop raising your voice. It is not my fault you got a mistress who also wanted to have a child! That is your own fault! I am fine with being held responsible for having King'ori, but I refuse to be crucified for that tart's bastard!

Oh, so you are still on your high horse? You queen of virtue!

Njogu, you are worrying me. You are looking deranged.

Deranged! You have not yet seen anything! King'ori hates me! The boy I brought up as my own flesh and blood hates me. I have no relationships with my family. You chased them away during our early years of marriage and I sat and watched them go! The woman I love is in jail for life! You have even destroyed the memory of what Nyambura and I had. I now will always have to wonder who fathered Njogu Jr. too! I am bound to you by bonds of blackmail! I have no friends. No one wants to be acquainted with a man who is so unfortunate. You know the only one silver lining in this dark cloud?

Please stop acting like this. You are frightening me.

If I am frightening you, then my job is complete. Ask me what the silver lining is!

W..Wha...What is the silver lining?

The silver lining is that someone cannot be killed twice.

You are frightening me! Stay away from me!

This Peris Wanjiru, does not exist.

Please, Njogu you are frightening me.

If you die today, who will look for you? Your children? Your husband? Your mother? No one will look for you. You are already dead!

Njogu, please....

Njogu grabbed Wambui by the neck. He began to squeeze like a maniac. Wambui struggled. She felt her airway compress and she struggled to get some air. The look on her eyes was at first one of bewilderment, followed by shock and eventually they were completely still – frozen in horror.

Njogu got on the phone and called Njoroge. He said, "It is complete. Come dispose of the goods." Njogu then made one other call and he said, "Yes, it is me. As we discussed you will deal with the man I told you about. Yes, the one from Kibera laini saba. Do it exactly two weeks from now. Yes, it has to look like an accident."

Njogu sat down and poured himself a drink of whisky as he waited for Njoroge.

The End

About the author

Ciku Kimeria lives and works in Kenya as a writer, blogger, and a communication consultant. In her free time, she enjoys writing and traveling. She holds a BSc in Management Science from the Massachusetts Institute of Technology (MIT).

For more about this author and to find future titles, please visit her website and travel blog at www.thekenyanexplorer.com. She can also be found on Twitter and Instagram as "cikucheru" and has the following facebook pages "Of goats and poisoned oranges", "thekenyanexplorer" and "Ciku Kimeria" author page. She can be reached via email on thekenyanexplorer@gmail.com

First published in December 2013
Third reprint (i.e. Fourth print) – February 2021

[i] Chamas predominantly started out as women's groups created by friends to help each other save and invest. Typically associated with women, but men in Kenya increasingly having their own chama groups
[ii] Tripe
[iii] Kikuyu word of endearment. Literally translates to "sweet orange"
[iv] Riff raff
[v] Land
[vi] Kenyan slang for unsuccessful attempts at job searching
[vii] Kenyan delicacy – roast goat
[viii] Githeri – A traditional Kikuyu meal primarily made of maize and beans
[ix] Mzungu is the Kiswahili word for white people but in this case directly refers to British colonialists
[x] Kenyan freedom fighter
[xi] Colloquial speech for a man who is controlled by his wife
[xii] Member of Parliament
[xiii] Kenyan colloquial term for an older woman who is dating a younger man and probably maintaining his lifestyle
[xiv] Made up term for an older woman who dates younger men that maintain her lifestyle
[xv] Gap between front teeth
[xvi] A particular illicit brew that has very high alcohol content, and has in the recent past led to hospitalizations, blindness and even death
[xvii] Kenyan tradition of community self-help events
[xviii] Dowry in the modern Kikuyu community is usually calculated in the cost of a certain number of goats. Historically it was paid in the form of goats, and the term "taking goats" is now synonymous with paying dowry for one's bride
[xix] The Kiswahili word for money
[xx] The Kikuyu naming norm is that the first born son and first born daughter are named after the man's parents, while the second born son and second born daughter are named after the woman's parents; however in the case of an unmarried

woman, the norm is to name her children after her parent's unless the man has shown clear intention to marry her

[xxi] "Who owns Nairobi?" It is a song about how Nairobi is ran/owned by certain individuals

[xxii] Minibuses that are one of the main forms of public transportation in Kenya

[xxiii] Large hand drawn cart used to transport medium sized luggage or produce and that is pushed by people